We'd gone about six hundred yards when we heard a hissing sound, followed by a loud crack and a sudden shriek. There were footsteps, not fifty feet away, and Maggie and I froze, holding our breaths, hiding behind a tree. There were rustling noises, and then absolutely nothing. I strained to listen, afraid to breathe, but the night had gone silent.

"What do you think that was?" Maggie whispered so softly that I could barely hear her. I touched my finger to her lips and shook my head. I had no idea. We stood there for what seemed an eternity, eyes straining against the dark. Finally I decided to move. We could either go back or go forward, but we couldn't stand there forever. I took one tentative step and then another, gaining confidence when no sound was made. Slowly, we began inching forward.

Suddenly, not twenty feet away, I sensed a movement. I turned to signal Maggie to stay put, but she'd already started toward the next tree. I turned back and saw a figure emerge, and with the faint light of the moon, I could just make out the form of a man, dressed in army fatigues, raising his hand toward Maggie. Sound exploded in a hiss from the end of his outstretched hand, and there was a distinct thwack as Maggie was spun around and slammed to the ground. The figure raced toward her and was about to fall upon her when I leaped.

2ND FIDDLE

A CASSIDY JAMES MYSTERY

by
KATE CALLOWAY

THE NAIAD PRESS, INC.
1997

Printed in the United States of America on acid-free paper
First Edition

Editor: Christine Cassidy
Cover designer: Bonnie Liss (Phoenix Graphics)
Typesetter: Sandi Stancil

Library of Congress Cataloging-in-Publication Data

Calloway, Kate. 1957 –
   Second fiddle : A Cassidy James mystery / by Kate Calloway.
      p.   cm.
   ISBN 1-56280-161-9
   I. Title.
PS3553.A4245S43   1996
813'.54—dc20
                                                    96-47130
                                                        CIP

In memory of Martha.

*Would that I could do
her true character justice.*

Acknowledgments

My heart-felt thanks to my friends and family who continue to support and encourage me. My special gratitude goes to those who volunteered, once again, to read and offer valuable feedback on this novel: Lyn, Linda, Carolyn, Murrell, Deva, and of course, Carol, who continues to be my greatest inspiration and support. Each offered unique and vital input, and somehow figured out a way to make it all sound positive. I'd also like to thank the two D.C.'s for sharing their knowledge of trees and boats, and J.C. for her willingness toward impromptu research. And finally, thanks to my editor, Christi Cassidy. With a name like Cassidy, how could she steer me wrong?

About the Author

Kate Calloway was born in 1957. She lives in Southern California with her lover and two cats. A teacher by day, a poet by night, she is really just a song-writer at heart. *Second Fiddle* is the second novel in the Cassidy James mystery series.

Chapter One

Sheets of rain pounded the windows, battering the glass in deafening waves. Douglas fir and cedar thrashed and bowed in the blustery wind, and the usually glassy lake had whitecaps rolling across the surface. I put another log on the fire. Even my cats, Panic and Gammon, had taken refuge from the raging storm, curled together in a single ball of spotted fur by the hearth. The lake had already risen several feet, and there was no sign of the rain letting up any time soon. Luckily, my cupboards were well stocked, so there was no danger of starving to death.

On the other hand, I might well die of sheer boredom if I couldn't get outside soon. It was almost June, and I was ready for summer.

Through the rain-streaked windows I could make out the shape of an approaching boat. Curious, I watched as it bobbed along the choppy surface, fighting its way through the rough water. The red cabin cruiser made several tentative passes before finally pulling up to my dock. I didn't recognize the boat, nor the two men draped in yellow rain slickers who struggled to secure it to the metal cleats on my dock. Through my binoculars, I could see them peering through the driving rain at my house. When they started to make their way up the ramp, I decided to check on my gun, which hung next to my purse in the clothes closet.

I carried the gun about as often as I did the purse, which was hardly ever. I'm not normally an alarmist, but the sight of two strange men approaching my house where I live alone, secluded in the woods, with no access road, made me a little nervous. The fact that we were in the middle of a raging storm, with the phone lines already down, made me think that this might be a good time to make sure the thing was loaded. It was.

"Can I help you?" I asked, opening the sliding glass door just far enough to stick my head out. My right hand was wrapped tightly around the butt of my .38, just out of view.

"We're looking for Cassidy James, the private investigator," the taller one shouted. They were both sopping wet, despite their slickers, and looked fairly harmless up close. Still, you never knew.

"And who are you?" I asked, eyeing them. The

2

taller one looked to be in his forties, the other one, who was shivering, seemed somewhat younger.

"We live here on the lake," the tall one said. "Over on Cedar Ridge. We need your help."

I'm a sucker for anyone who says they need me. Sure they could have been cold-blooded killers for all I knew, but one little mention of needing my help and I threw open the door and let them in.

"Thank you," the younger one said, stepping into the entryway. "I was afraid you weren't going to let us in. Is that a gun?" His blue eyes widened with alarm.

"Uh, just a precaution," I said, feeling ridiculous. Now that I could see their faces, I felt sure they were not out to harm me. Still, that's probably what people had said when Jeffrey Dahmer had invited them over for drinks. I stashed the gun in the closest drawer and showed them where to hang their wet coats.

The taller one, who looked as if he had stock in Nautilus, smiled warmly. "I'm Towne Meyers," he said, combing his black hair back with his fingers before extending his hand. "And this is Rick." I shook hands and was glad to note that both of them had nice, firm grips. Not the killer grip that some men insist upon, but no wimpy dead-fish grip either. I like to think I can tell a lot about a guy by his handshake. Sometimes, I'm right.

"We're sorry to barge in on you like this without calling or anything, but the phones are down, and we needed to talk to you right away. We found you in the phone book. You *are* a private investigator, aren't you?" Rick spoke rapidly, his soft voice strained with worry.

3

"Yes, I am," I answered. "Why don't you gentlemen come on in and get warm by the fire. I'll put some water on the stove, and then you can tell me all about it. You look like you could both use something hot."

They followed me into the living area which was really one big room. The kitchen opened into the dining room which opened into the living room. There were no dividing walls, making conversation from room to room possible. I filled the copper kettle from the faucet and got down three cups. "Tea or coffee?" I asked. "Or something stronger?"

When I turned around, Rick had kneeled down by the fire and was stroking the cats awake.

"Oh, my God!" he said. "They are too cute. I love them. What kind are they?"

"Their daddy was a Bengal and their mother was an Egyptian Mau," I told him. "They were bred for their spots. The portly one is Gammon. That's Panic with the loud purr. Usually they're running around tearing up the house. Today they're hiding from the storm."

Rick lifted Panic onto his shoulder and began stroking her long, silky tail. I could hear the purr all the way across the room.

"Oh, dear," Towne said, playing with his moustache. "Now he'll want one."

"Feel her fur," Rick demanded, turning his shoulder so Towne could stroke Panic's back. "Have you ever felt anything so luxurious in all your life?"

"You see?" Towne said to me, laughing. "I knew it. I just hope you don't have a cow out back. Soon he'll be wanting one of those, too."

Rick feigned a pout and walked over to the

4

kitchen. "Tea for me, and since you offered, I will have just a splash of something in it. Brandy? Or whiskey. Whatever you have. It's not just the cold. This whole thing has got me all jittery."

I dug in the cupboard and found a bottle of Jim Beam. "For you too?" I asked Towne.

"Oh, why not?" he said. "I've already taken the day off work. I don't make a habit of drinking before five, but this hasn't been an ordinary day — or week, for that matter. Just a dollop."

I poured a splash of whiskey in all three cups, squeezed a bit of lemon in each, and poured in steaming hot water, letting the tea bags steep until the water was a deep, rich brown. While we were waiting, I studied the two men, who in turn walked around examining my house. Towne was the larger of the two, with a weight lifter's body and a face that had been ravaged by childhood acne. His eyes were warm and intelligent, and he had a lopsided smile that saved his face from being homely.

Rick was Towne's physical opposite. Slender to the point of almost being frail, Rick was light-complected with sandy blond hair and blue eyes. If he hadn't been so pretty, he could have been my twin brother. His eyes sparkled, and his smile was contagious. He had no trouble making himself at home as he toured my living room. Like a child, he seemed to find delight in even the smallest objects. Clearly, Panic was smitten, and even Gammon had begun following Rick around, swatting at his heels until he hefted her up too and carried her on his other shoulder. I don't always trust my own instincts but I've never known a cat to be wrong.

I gave the men their mugs and sat down in my

favorite blue swivel chair. They settled onto the couch and the cats snuggled onto Rick's lap. It felt like one big, happy family even though I had no idea who these men were or what they wanted. The rain continued to pelt the window, and the fire crackled comfortingly. I waited for one of them to speak up and finally Towne blurted, "We're being blackmailed."

"I see."

"We have no idea who it is!" Rick added. "It's obviously someone in town. But we've been so careful!"

"What Rick's trying to say," Towne interrupted, "is that we've tried very hard to conceal the nature of our relationship. Our particular lifestyle might be frowned upon by some people, especially in a place like Cedar Hills. And now someone has not only found us out but has threatened to expose us publicly."

"What Towne's trying to say," Rick said, mimicking his friend with a wry grin, "is that we're gay. I hope that doesn't offend you. I know some people can't stand the thought of being in the same room with a couple of queers. Afraid it's contagious or something. You're not like that, are you?"

I laughed at his worried expression. "I think you're safe with me," I said, adding, "I'm a lesbian."

The look of relief and surprise on both their faces was almost comical.

"Thank God," Towne said, taking a shallow sip of his tea. "At least we don't have to tiptoe around that subject."

"Can you believe it?" Rick said, clearly pleased.

"The only private investigator in the book turns out to be one of us."

"So tell me about the blackmail," I said, smiling at their reactions, "and start from the beginning."

The two of them talked, interrupting each other often, which didn't seem to bother either of them. It was like listening to a duet, impossible at times to separate the melody from the harmony.

Towne worked as an accountant in Kings Harbor, about ten miles south of Cedar Hills. Rick was a fairly successful artist. The two of them had been together sixteen years, a minor miracle for gay men in the Nineties. That they were both alive in this decade was itself a miracle. Their early commitment to monogamy may have not only saved their marriage, but probably their lives as well.

They'd finally earned enough money to buy their house on the lake two summers ago. The house had belonged to Towne's uncle, who'd sold it to Towne. He'd had better offers but he'd wanted to keep it in the family. Rick and Towne still had their house in Kings Harbor and during the rainy season they sometimes stayed in town, but whenever they could, they spent their time at the lake.

A week ago, they'd received a threatening letter. Rick had gone down to the dock to get the mail and found among the bills an envelope addressed "Queers." With a sick feeling, he opened the envelope and read the enclosed letter.

"It's right here if you want to read it," he said, handing me the typed sheet.

The first thing I noticed was that it appeared to

have been done on a word processor, which I doubted very many people in Cedar Hills owned. On the other hand, the local library had recently purchased a few Macintosh computers, so anyone now had access to one. The message was brief and to the point:

"Get out of town. Now. If we wanted to live with faggots, we'd move to San Francisco. Don't wait for this to get ugly. It will be your loss. I'm sure your boss at MacIntyre's Accounting Services would be very interested in some of the stories I could tell him. And it sure would be a shame if something happened to those pretty little pictures you fruit loops like to paint. Can I make myself clearer? Scram!"

The letter wasn't signed.

"You said this was in your mailbox. But there's no stamp or address." I turned the letter over. There were no stains or smudges.

"I guess it's safe to assume that someone drove by the boat dock and put it in our mailbox. We get our mail by boat like almost everyone else without road access," Towne said. "Obviously it's someone close by, but that's what's so baffling. Absolutely no one knows us in town. We do our shopping and banking in Kings Harbor. Even Gus Townsend, the marina owner, doesn't know where I work. How could someone know so much about us when no one really knows us?" His intelligent eyes were troubled, and he took a long drink of his tea.

"We try hard not to offend anyone," Rick said, using his finger to swirl the lemon in his cup. "The reason we love living out here is because our house is so private. We certainly don't hold hands or anything in public. I don't see how anyone could even know we're gay, let alone that I'm an artist. It's downright spooky."

This may have been true, but the way gossip traveled in Cedar Hills, if even one person knew, there was a good chance half the town did too.

As the storm continued to rage outside, I took notes, asking anything I could think of that might turn out to be useful, but there really wasn't much to go on. In addition to the letter, they'd received two calls, the most recent coming that morning just a few hours before the phones on the lake went dead. In both cases the message was simple: "Get out of town, fags," the voice had warned. It had been male, but beyond that, the voice was unremarkable. Even before the most recent call, they had talked about going to the police but finally agreed to hire a private investigator.

I found myself totally charmed by these two men. Towne seemed so strong and sensible, and Rick was funny and sensitive. They complemented each other beautifully, and it was clear they were a good match. Unfortunately, someone in Cedar Hills didn't seem to agree.

"Have you seen anyone following you? Noticed a car or boat hanging around?"

"Believe me, ever since we got the letter, we've been looking over our shoulders. Neither of us has noticed anything strange," Towne said.

"Have you considered changing your number?"

"What would be the point?" Rick asked. "They'd just send another letter. Or worse, pay a visit." He had a point.

"What strikes me as unusual," I said, "is that they're not asking for money. And the letter does say 'we' so I'm assuming there is more than one person involved. Usually, blackmail is used for profit. But whoever this is doesn't ask for money to keep your secret. They simply want you to leave town. Which is strange since, as you say, people hardly ever see you together. I think once we figure out why they want you to leave, we should be able to get to the bottom of this."

I didn't tell them that I had absolutely no idea where to start. I wasn't too worried though, because these things usually came to me at odd times, like in the shower or cooking dinner. In the last year, I'd begun to trust my instincts and to not panic when I didn't have any. Things would fall into place once I started nosing around, I told myself, and smiled at them reassuringly so they wouldn't detect my own self-doubts.

We made arrangements for me to meet Rick at their house the next day after I'd had a chance to draw up an estimate and some sort of plan. The rain had finally begun to let up and off to the west, just over Cedar Hills Ridge, a few patches of aqua could be seen between the steely clouds. Rick took this as a good omen.

"Look!" he said as they got their coats. "It's starting to clear. I feel better already. I'm so glad we decided to go with a private detective. Especially you. It's the first time in a week I've felt this good."

"That's probably just the whiskey," Towne teased.

Even though we'd just met, I felt as if I'd known the men for ages. And what surprised me more was that I really liked them. I tended to be pretty picky about who I called friends, but I had a good feeling about both Rick and Towne.

10

Donning my rain jacket I walked them down to the dock and helped them shove off. It was barely drizzling but the wind was still fierce and quite nippy. I hugged my jacket closer as I watched their red boat battle the choppy waves across the cove and disappear from view.

Back in the house, I threw another log on the fire and decided it really wasn't too early for a glass of wine. I had a few bottles left of a good Oregon Pinot Gris I'd discovered, and I figured getting new clients was good enough reason to celebrate. In truth, I was more excited about the prospect of two new friends than the case itself. I sat by the fire, sipping my wine, with Panic and Gammon for company.

I'd only been a licensed detective for less than a year, but after solving my first case, it seemed everyone in town knew who I was and what I did for a living. And surprisingly enough, I'd been kept busy through the winter. A couple of my clients had been wealthy lake-house owners on the verge of divorce, but some were the relatively poor town folk. I'd spent two whole weeks following a man whose wife was sure he was cheating on her, only to discover that he was actually building her a cabin on the lake as a surprise. I'd helped track down a run-away teen who'd made it all the way to Gold Beach, and most recently, I'd discovered which employee at McGregor's was pilfering small change from the cash drawer. Most of the locals tended to pay me in barter, which was fine with me since in reality I wasn't hurting financially, thanks to a generous insurance policy from my first lover's death. In fact, I sometimes preferred the barter system. I'd gotten my dock and decks pressure-washed and enough firewood chopped for the next winter that way. And I knew that if it weren't for the barter system, I might not be in business at all. My clients came to me by word of mouth, but every now and then someone found me through the Yellow Pages as Rick and Towne had done.

All in all, it was a satisfactory way to make a living and had I not been pining away for the woman of my dreams, who had spent the winter and now the spring in Southern California, it might have been a nice year.

As always, thinking of Erica made my heart ache. My first client, Erica Trinidad, was one of the most beautiful women I'd ever known. She awakened feelings in me I thought had long since died along with my first lover some three years earlier. That Erica could bring me to such depths of passion both terrified and excited me. From the very first kiss we had been intense and passionate lovers. Just when I was beginning to think I'd found a second lifetime partner, she slipped away.

"It's something I have to pursue, Cass," she'd said that morning, her piercing blue eyes alive with excitement. "A chance to have one of my novels on screen! And she wants me to co-write the screenplay. I'll be working directly with probably the best female producer in the business. It's not about the money. It's a chance to break into a whole new field!" Erica's face was even more beautiful than usual, as she went on and on about her new career opportunities. I sat at the kitchen table, nodding, smiling, listening, waiting for her to get to the part where

12

she asked me to come with her. Nine months later, I was still waiting for that part.

At first, she called regularly, and we'd made plans for when we'd next see each other. But she never directly invited me to visit, and the calls had become less frequent. When she did call, there wasn't much to talk about. The truth was, our time together had been spent mostly in bed, and we hadn't had enough time to build common experiences.

But it was the experiences we did share that were driving me crazy. Having managed to repress whatever sexual feelings I'd had after Diane died, I'd been completely unprepared for the way my body responded to Erica. She had waltzed into my life, ignited a raging fire and then left me to deal with the smoldering coals. They'd begun to die down some, but I feared the slightest breeze would fan them right back to life. I was a walking sexual time bomb. I had sex on the brain. Face it, I told myself as I got up to pour another glass of wine, I was horny.

When the phone rang around six-thirty, I rushed to answer it. It had been weeks since I'd heard from Erica but this was the time of day she sometimes called. I tried to hide my disappointment when my best friend's voice came over the line.

"It's about time, Cass. I've been trying your number for hours. What's the deal? You forget to pay your phone bill?"

"It's this storm. The whole lake's been without service all day. They must have just got them working. Looks like the storm's finally passing too. What's up?"

Martha's voice was rich and warm, and there was always a hint of laughter just under the surface. For a cop, she had a remarkably good sense of humor. She could come on tough when she needed to, but deep down she was really a teddy bear.

"I'm trying to find a fourth for dinner Saturday night. Women on Top is putting on this dinner dance at the Regency Inn, and Cindy's date had a family emergency. She's had the tickets for months and hates for them to go to waste. I told her I'd ask my best friend, who hasn't been out of the house in ages, if she'd condescend to joining three gorgeous females for a night on the town. How about it?"

"You're not setting me up for another blind date, are you?" I asked, thinking that that's exactly what Martha was doing. When Erica's absence had extended into spring, Martha had started a not-so-subtle campaign to introduce me to every available lesbian along the Oregon coast. The funny part was, Martha seemed to have dated most of them herself. But I had never shared her need for numerous conquests. I'd had one perfect relationship. That's more than most people ever get. Meeting Erica had made me think that maybe I'd get a chance at a second one. Now I wasn't so sure.

Martha was laughing. "I swear to God, Cass. Cindy is already involved. No set-up this time. Honest. We really would just enjoy your company. You can drive your own car and leave as early as you want. How about it?"

Martha was hard to resist.

"What time?" I asked, secretly warming to the idea. It *had* been a long time since I'd been out on the town, as Martha put it.

"Come by my house around five. We'll have a glass of wine and then head over. I like to make a fashionable entrance." She was clearly pleased that I'd succumbed so easily. We chatted a bit more and I told her the barest details of my new case. When I mentioned Rick's name, Martha's voice rose two decibels.

"Rick Parker? The artist? I love his paintings. My old therapist had his stuff hanging all over her office. All I had to do was look at them and all my deep, dark secrets would come pouring out. I'd love to meet him."

"They both seem really nice," I said. "I think you'd like them. But I wish I felt better about the case. To tell you the truth, I don't have the slightest idea where to start."

"Oh, Cassidy. You say that every single time. And you always figure out where to start. I bet by this time tomorrow night, you'll have the whole damn thing solved."

As usual, Martha's laughter made me feel light-hearted and happy. We said good-bye and I decided to do something about dinner. Any more wine on an empty stomach would be dangerous.

One of the great things about living alone is you can eat whatever and whenever you want. I like to cook and I like to eat. It's a miracle I'm as thin as I am. Martha, who constantly battles her weight, would kill for my metabolism.

I poked through the refrigerator until I found what I wanted. I sliced a sourdough baguette into six rounds, spooned a dollop of olive oil on each one and spread on a thick layer of goat cheese. On top of this I placed an oily, sun-dried tomato and sprinkled basil on three of them and tarragon on the others. I popped these into the oven, placed a bunch of Thompson seedless grapes on a plate, and poured another glass of wine, sipping while I waited. I didn't exactly have all the food groups covered, but what the hell. I was a thirty-one-year-old lesbian private detective and I could eat what I damn well pleased.

Chapter Two

The storm had continued to pelt rain against my bedroom window off and on all night, but by Friday morning, the sky was a brilliant blue and the sun was shining. It had been over a week since I'd gotten a good walk in and I was tired of the stationary bicycle in my den as my sole means of exercise. I threw on a pair of what I thought of as my "town sweats" as opposed to my "work-in-the-yard sweats" or my "lounge-around-the-house sweats." I had lots of other clothes in my wardrobe to choose from, mind you, but one of the perks of being your own boss is that you can dress however you please. There was no one I cared to impress that morning, so I dressed for comfort.

Gammon and Panic were eager to get outside and I tried to appease them by dragging an old string with a sock tied on the end of it up and down the hallway, but they were having none of it. I gave them each a chicken-flavored Pounce, which brought on a burst of purring from Gammon, who was something of a glutton. When I finally made my exit, I had to slither past them, blocking what would have been a hasty escape.

"I'll take you for a ride in the boat later," I told them. They acted like they understood me, which I knew was far-fetched, but maybe something in my tone held a promise of good things to come, because once I was out the glass door, they hopped up onto one of the wide window sills and sat grooming each other in the sun.

It took me about ten minutes to remove the canvas boat cover, fold it up properly and stow it beneath the seats. My boat is a sky-blue, open bow Sea Swirl, just the right size for life on the lake. While the engine was warming up, I checked the flower barrels lining the back of my dock. Most of the begonias and geraniums had survived the winter and those that hadn't, I'd replaced in April. They'd taken quite a beating from this last storm though, and I was concerned that the delicate buds were damaged. Maybe with a few days of sunshine, I thought, they'd pull through.

It's about a ten-minute ride to town unless I take my time, putt-putting along, going around the island, hugging the shore. But that morning, with the early morning sun beating down on me, I felt like racing across the water, feeling the spray of the water, the exhilaration of speed. I passed a few fishermen on the way and made a point of steering clear of their boats so as not to inundate them with my wake. They waved their thanks and I waved back, feeling ridiculously young and happy.

The Cedar Hills Marina sits at the juncture of Rainbow Lake and Rainbow Creek which runs a mile west to the ocean. The creek is chock full of steelhead and salmon, and in the days when it was still legal to fish it, people came from miles around whenever the salmon ran. Recent depletions in the salmon population had put a temporary ban on the fishing, although every time I'd taken a canoe down the creek, I'd seen plenty of anglers hidden along the banks, skirting the law for the thrill of hooking one of the giant kings. That morning, as I eased my boat into a vacant slip, I noticed Tommy, the marina attendant, trying his luck from the last dock. Technically, he was still in the lake, but he was casting close enough to the mouth of the creek that if Sheriff Booker caught him, he'd give him hell. I liked Booker a lot, and we'd worked together a couple of times. The only time I'd ever seen him really get mad was when someone ignored the fishing laws. Booker liked Tommy but that wouldn't prevent him from chewing him out big time if he caught him pulling a salmon out of the mouth of the creek. I waved to Tommy, who put down his rod somewhat guiltily and came bouncing over.

"Hey, Cassidy. You been hiding out? Ain't seen you around in forever," he said, his elfin face breaking into a grin. He was a cute kid, small and wiry, but with surprising strength for his size. He walked on the balls of his feet, leaning forward, and when he smiled, his whole face got into the act. His bright blue eyes were small but full of mischief, and he reminded me of the proverbial cat who'd just had his first taste of canary.

"How you doing, Tommy?" I climbed out of the boat. "You trying to tempt fate, sneaking fish out of the creek like that? Good thing it was me that caught you and not Sheriff Booker. I think he charged the last guy five hundred dollars." I was making that part up, but Tommy's eyes widened and his already pink face turned red.

"Aw, Cass, I wasn't fishing. I was just practicing casting my new bass lure. She's a beaut. Won her off of Jess Martin playin' poker last week. We run out of money and started bettin' all kinds of crazy stuff. Got me a hardly ever used putter too. Gonna learn me how to play golf this summer. You wanna teach me?"

Every now and then Tommy came up with something that was dangerously close to a come-on, and he always looked so miserably embarrassed afterwards that I usually went easy on him. I wasn't publicly out as a lesbian in Cedar Hills, but both Sheriff Booker and my friend Jess Martin knew, and I was pretty sure that if they knew, so did half the town. There was no such thing as a secret in Cedar Hills, but then maybe this particular secret was something people just didn't want to talk about. Still, I was pretty sure Tommy must have known, but just in case, I decided to nix any romantic illusions he might harbor.

"I'm afraid my teaching days are over, Tommy. I

20

had enough of that teaching junior high school years ago." I intentionally made myself sound ancient, and for the hundredth time wondered just how old little Tommy really was. Somewhere between eighteen and twenty-five, I figured, but he hadn't changed one iota in the four years I'd lived on the lake, and he could easily pass for younger. I could see from his expression that I had hurt his feelings. "So, did you leave Jess with any belongings at all?" I asked, trying to lighten things up.

"Well, yeah, actually," he said, grinning again. "He's now the proud owner of an old broken-down weed eater that I rescued out of the trash bin about a month ago. Don't even know why I took it, but you shoulda seen ol' Jess's eyes light up when I threw it in. Woulda thought he'd won the lottery. He probably will get it fixed though. That Jess can fix anything!"

"He probably will," I said, heading up the ramp to the street. I waved good-bye to him, wishing I could have been more up-front. I didn't like being afraid of exposing myself. There were plenty of homophobic weirdos out there, and the problem was, you didn't know who they were until they turned on you. I thought of Rick and Towne and wondered again who would be so full of hate as to threaten to expose them if they didn't leave town. It just sounded too pat, I thought. There had to be more to it, and I was anxious to find out what it was.

Cedar Hills is situated on the edge of Rainbow Lake with neat little houses dotting the tree-lined streets. It's not a prosperous town, although at its peak, when railroads were the main means of transportation and the forestry service had not yet stripped the land of the giant cedar and Douglas fir, it had been a booming resort spot. The replacement trees — fir, cedar and alder — have all grown in but are only a third as large as their predecessors. The town still gets its share of tourists during peak fishing seasons, but the people who live in the town are for the most part refugees from the cities, more interested in living in peace and beauty than in being upwardly mobile.

Out on the lake, the houses are owned by the richer city folk, who come in the summers from all over the country. The townspeople tolerate the lake-house owners because of the revenue they generate, but they tend to keep their distance. I was one of the rich city folk who had bought a slice of paradise out there, but unlike most of them, I decided to live and work here full time, giving me the honorary status of a real Oregonian. Not that anyone forgot I came from Southern California. But they didn't rub it in as much as they could have, and with each winter I stayed on, the respect they doled out seemed to increase.

Since becoming a full-fledged private eye, I'd had to alter my walking route. No longer could I stroll through the town street by street, enjoying the changing scenery. Too many people would stop me along the way to chat, hoping to find new tidbits of gossip, and I could never work up a decent sweat. My new route took me down Main Street, which was unavoidable, but just after I passed Jess Martin's house, I cut through an old gravel alley and headed over to North Fork Road. Beside the road was a dirt path which led all the way to Eagle Lake. Once there, I switched to an asphalt bike path that went all the way around Eagle Lake, which was a little sister to Rainbow Lake, connected by a navigable stream.

That morning every bird within ten miles must have been celebrating the end of the storm. Their songs filled the sky as I walked among the trees enjoying the fresh scent of newly washed greenery. Twice on my path I startled a deer, the second one just a fawn with light golden spots on its rear, and huge liquid eyes. We stared at each other for a full minute before it bounded off into the woods, back to its mother. In all, it couldn't have been a more invigorating walk, and by the time I wound my way back to town, I not only had worked up quite a sweat, but I was ravenous.

By far, the Cedar Hills Lodge had the best breakfast in town. I tried to limit my visits, because even *my* metabolism wouldn't withstand the cholesterol intake for long, but every now and then I just couldn't resist. I asked for a patio table overlooking the lake, knowing it would be too warm inside after my walk. Jess Martin's most recent girlfriend was waiting tables that morning and she brought me a whole pot of coffee with the menu. I pretended to consider the options, knowing full well I'd order what I always did, and when I did, I caught Lilly mouthing my order as I said it. When I laughed, she turned red-faced and then laughed too.

"Predictable as everyone else in this town," she said. "You want the links or the patties?" For a moment, I considered going out on a limb and ordering something different, but I really liked the sausage patties and I'd be damned if I'd let Lilly bully me into ordering something I didn't want.

When I told her, she smiled condescendingly and turned on her heels, nodding all the way back into the restaurant.

"Lilly giving you a hard time?" a gravelly voice boomed behind me, making me jump. I looked up and smiled at Sheriff Tom Booker, who must have slipped out the door when Lilly went in. His silver hair and mustache framed his handsome tan face, making him look, as always, like a cowboy movie star. He pulled up a chair and slid into it, helping himself to some coffee.

"She says I'm predictable," I complained. "But damn it, I like sausage patties. Why should I order links when I prefer the patties?"

Booker laughed and held up his hands in mock surrender. "Hey, I'm a patty man myself. Wouldn't dream of ordering links. Don't pay any attention to her. She's having a bad hair day. She and Jess kind of broke up last night, so she's taking it out on the customers. Where've you been, anyway?"

"They broke up? Damn. I thought Jess was finally going to settle down. Besides, little Jessie could use some stability in her life. What happened?"

"Actually, I think Lilly wants to settle down. It's Jess that called it off. He said things were moving too fast, and he wanted to slow things down some. The way I figure, it's either right or it isn't. I mean, if you love someone, you want to be with them plain and simple. You don't need more time to think it over. Jess does want to find someone, but I think he knows in his heart that Lilly isn't the one."

Just then Lilly burst through the swinging door, using her hips for leverage, and banged her way to the table.

"You eating again?" she said to Booker, clanging my plates on the table.

"No ma'am," Booker said. "I ate so much the first time, I can barely waddle as it is. Gonna have to go on a diet, you keep feeding me like this. I would take some cream in this coffee though, when you get a chance." Booker was at his charming best, but Lilly was only slightly appeased. She left with a harumph, reappearing a minute later with a silver cream pitcher which she sloshed onto the red checkered table cloth as she set it down. No apology, no good-bye, no nothing. Maybe it was just as well they broke up, I thought. Little Jessie didn't need a cranky replacement-mom who threw temper tantrums.

While I downed my sausage, eggs and biscuits, the sheriff filled me in on the local gossip. It seemed everyone was in a lather trying to figure out who Buddy Drake, the lake-route mail carrier, was having an affair with. That he was involved with someone was not in doubt. After years of personal neglect, Buddy had started grooming himself. Last month, he'd shaved for the first time since anyone in Cedar Hills had known him, giving his face a two-toned hue because the skin beneath the beard was pale as a baby's butt, while his nose and upper cheeks were deeply tanned. And then, last week, he'd taken off his baseball cap and hadn't put it back on. Buddy without his cap was like my breakfast without sausage patties. Unthinkable. And then, the real clincher. On Sunday, Buddy Drake had gone to church.

"You've got to be kidding!" I said, choking on my biscuit. "Church? What on earth for?"

"Well, either the lady of his desires is also a

church-goer, or what he's up to is so bad that it requires repentance. Half the people in town will be at church this Sunday just to see who else is there, looking for Buddy's sweetheart. The new minister is going to think he's converted the whole town!" He laughed and helped himself to a bite of one of my sausage patties.

"I hate to point this out," I said, "but if half the people in town are there, no one will be able to narrow it down much. They'll all be pointing fingers at one another. Any idea who the lucky lady might be?"

"I'd have to guess it's someone along his mail route, which means someone out on the lake. It's sure not anyone local, or we'd know already. It seems to me Buddy started sprucing himself up right after that Walter Trinidad case last summer. Then he kind of went back to his old ways. Now it's happening again. I'd guess one of those rich lake-house ladies has come back for the season. Kind of early though. Unless she was in an awful hurry to see old Buddy."

We amused ourselves with the thought of Buddy, just over five feet tall, and some regal, wealthy widow towering over him while they shared a few stolen minutes in her boat house, with his motor running, the mail waiting to be delivered.

"You working any interesting cases lately?" he asked when we'd finally quit laughing.

I told him about the blackmail case, leaving out the names and the fact that the victims were gay.

"If they don't want money, what is it they're asking for?" he asked, puzzled. Sheriff Booker liked discussing my cases because they were generally more interesting than his own. As the town sheriff, his main job was keeping law and order on the lake. He made sure people didn't speed through the channels, litter on the lake or fish without licenses, even though officially that job belonged to the game warden. But since the game warden seldom made it out this far, and since the sheriff was a nut about protecting the wildlife and environment, he took it upon himself to patrol the fishermen. In all, it was a cushy job, and one that many a Kings Harbor cop coveted. On the other hand, people came to me with things they didn't want the police to get involved in. It tended to be mundane stuff, but next to Booker's speeding tickets, my cases seemed almost adventurous. After years of checking boat registrations, Sheriff Booker longed for a little action. Of course, we'd both had plenty of that on my first case, when a band of neo-Nazi teens had gone on a rampage, and Booker and I had solved the case together. But since then, things had been pretty slow for the sheriff.

"They want the victims to leave town," I said. "That was the only demand."

"Why?" he asked. "What's in it for them? And what makes you think there's more than one blackmailer?"

"It's kind of a hate-motivated crime," I said. " 'You're bringing down the neighborhood' kind of thing. Something in the note suggests there's more than one of them."

"Well," he said, stroking his silver mustache thoughtfully, "I guess it's possible. I suppose if someone were trying to sell their house, for example, and they thought the neighbors were so undesirable as to bring down the sale value of the house, that might make sense. It's just that I've never known a blackmail case to be about anything besides money."

"So maybe I should start by looking at the neighbors," I said.

"The thing is, you've got to ask yourself, who will profit if they leave? Unless of course, it really is a hate crime. Then you might as well throw logic right out the door. Like those crazy boys out to kill Californians. Now that was sick," he said, referring to my first case again. People in Cedar Hills were still talking about it as if it were yesterday, and I knew that no matter how many future cases I'd solve, I'd forever be known by some as the lady who caught the California Killers. And there were some, I suspected, who thought I'd caught the boys a tad too soon. Californians in general did not seem to be overly adored in Oregon.

"Well, I'll never figure it out if I don't get started." I pushed my chair back and tossed a five on the table. Maybe the tip would cheer Lilly up.

"Let me know if I can help," he said. "Things have been pretty slow around here. I could use some excitement."

We shook hands, and I left him there to finish the coffee, looking out at the lake, a wistful expression on his face.

Chapter Three

By the time I'd managed to coax Panic and Gammon into the boat it was early afternoon. They'd been ecstatic to get outside, and they spent a good deal of time chasing butterflies and bees across the front lawn. It was good to watch them romp, and I spent the time messing with my flower pots on the front deck, wiping rainwater off the chairs, re-hanging the wind chimes which had been blown off their hook, and in general cleaning up after the storm. When at last they'd hopped up into the bow of my boat, I took off across the lake, going putt-putt speed so the two of them could look down into the water as we cruised. The sun was actually warm, a wonderful change from the recent cold front, and I was in no hurry to get over to Rick and Towne's.

Rainbow Lake is a huge tangle of legs and arms, with islands here and there, and dozens of private coves and peninsulas. It took me two years to really know the lake, and many a fisherman has gotten lost, especially when the fog rolls in off the ocean in early summer. After four years though, I knew every nook and cranny of the lake, so I took my time, hugging the shore, going the long way around the island across from my house until at last I could see the giant red cedars on top of Cedar Ridge. They were the last reminder of a previous lifetime, huge and proud, towering over the lake. I motored straight for the ridge and then followed the peninsula south, counting docks once I reached the inhabited area.

They'd said it was the fourth house from the top of the ridge, and when I pulled up to the dock, I noticed the mailbox, their names boldly printed on it, nailed to the edge of the dock. "Parker Meyers" was all it said, which could have been one man's name instead of two men's last names. And the house itself, as Rick had said, was extremely private. It sat well back from the water, surrounded by trees. The second story may have had a view, but it was as if they'd intentionally let the berry bushes, shrubbery and trees grow high, seemingly sacrificing the view for their privacy.

I told Panic and Gammon to stay put, having no idea if they would or not, and started the long climb up the formidable staircase to their house. I was winded by the time I reached the front deck. When I turned back toward the lake, I was surprised to find that they did in fact have a stupendous view. They had achieved the best of both worlds: to see and not be seen. And it was clear that whoever was bothered by their gayness hadn't just tooled by in their boat and stumbled upon the two men embracing. Even if someone tried, I doubted they could see much from the water. Whoever knew Rick and Towne were gay knew it some other way.

Rick came to the door and waved me in, a paintbrush in his left hand and a smile on his face. He was in a paint-covered smock, his blond hair tousled, a dab of blue paint on his cheek. He had a careless, natural beauty and seemed either unaware of it, or unimpressed by it. He led me through a bright, open kitchen to a sunroom which had been transformed into his studio. Light came pouring in the windows and the walls were covered with what must have been Rick's paintings. Bright splashes of color filled each canvas with impressionistic fields of flowers, sailboats in aqua bays, young girls in giant hats, and everywhere, tons and tons of flowers. I loved them.

"I'm almost done here and then we can go out on the deck," he said, squinting with determination at the easel in front of him. "Feel free to look around." Like the others, the canvas he was working on was filled with dazzling color, giant flowers that seemed to be nearly iridescent, a yellow and black bumblebee drinking greedily from the nectar of a bluebell.

I watched for a moment while he painted, his left hand making deft, sure strokes, his tongue sticking out the corner of his mouth in fierce concentration. Fearing that my watching him might be bothersome,

31

I eased out of the room and wandered around the house, gazing at the many paintings hanging throughout. The subjects varied, but the style was distinct; bright, vivid and pulsing with life. Martha had said she'd told all her deep, dark secrets looking at these paintings and I could understand why. They inspired trust, as if the artist had just told you a secret, shared an incredibly personal intimacy, and you felt compelled to do the same. They were intense without being obvious. Subtle strength. Like Rick himself, I thought suddenly. Real beauty does not require flaunting.

I felt instantly at home in the open-beamed, spacious rooms. Light streamed in everywhere, and like me, Rick and Towne weren't big on window coverings. I wondered if they closed the blinds at night.

I stepped out the sliding glass door to the back deck. No other houses could be seen from the porch, but I was surprised to see a dirt road about twenty feet straight across from their house. Rick had said they didn't have road access.

I walked out to the road and peered in both directions. I could just barely make out the yard of the next house to the north toward Cedar Ridge. To the south, I could tell where the next house was, but couldn't see more than the chimney jutting between the tall trees. Even if Rick and Towne spent a lot of time in their back yard, which I doubted, there was no way the neighbors could see them except if they happened to walk by on the road. I wondered again about that road. It obviously hadn't been used in some time, but even with the heavy growth crowding one side, it could have easily been made passable.

People paid a lot of money for houses with road access although I knew that some people, myself included, preferred the privacy that boat access allowed. It was possible, I supposed, that the people on Cedar Ridge had opted to not use the road even though it was there.

But even if all the neighbors used boat access only, maybe one of them liked to take leisurely strolls in the evenings, perhaps getting an eyeful of Rick and Towne in the process. And maybe that person was a homophobic nutcase who'd decided to clean up the neighborhood. Pure speculation, I knew, but I'd definitely have to check out the neighbors.

When I went back inside, Rick was carrying two glasses and an ice bucket with a bottle of white wine, out onto the front deck.

"Just grab that tray, if you would," he called over his shoulder. I picked up a tray with what looked suspiciously like crab-stuffed mushrooms and something resembling goose liver paté. I dipped a quick finger into the paté and confirmed my suspicions.

"My God," I said, joining him on the deck. "When did you have time to do all this? In between paintings?"

Rick laughed, pouring us each a half-glass of Fumé Blanc.

"I love to cook!" he exclaimed. "I put this together this morning first thing and then went to work on my painting. It just needed the final touches. What do you think?"

I popped a mushroom into my mouth, groaned with pleasure and sipped the wine. "I don't know what I love more, your paintings or your cooking. You've got to meet my friend Martha. She's already

33

in love with your paintings and when she finds out you can cook, she'll flip!" I told him about Martha's therapist having his paintings all over her office, and he nearly choked on his mushroom.

"Don't tell me!" he said. "Your friend's therapist is Doctor Carradine. Am I right?"

When I nodded, he started to sing the Disney song about it being a small world after all. He couldn't carry a tune, and I found myself laughing.

"I'm serious," he said. "Doctor Carradine was my therapist for two years. I was half in love with her. I was trying to deal with losing so many friends to AIDS, and Towne convinced me to try a therapist. It was the best money I ever spent. I stayed on long after I needed to, because I liked her so much. She didn't buy any of my paintings until after I stopped seeing her, but she's been a faithful customer ever since. Is your friend Martha still seeing her?"

"No. It was a short-term thing," I said, helping myself to another cracker and thinking back to Martha's ordeal.

She had only been a cop for about a year when she'd been forced to shoot some guy holding up a liquor store. He had come out shooting and Martha had no choice but to return fire. He was killed instantly. Outwardly, Martha had handled it like a pro. But inside, she'd been really messed up. The department had a shrink for that sort of thing but Martha couldn't open up to him. Finally, she sought out Dr. Carradine on her own, and like Rick, had stayed with her long after she'd gotten past the shooting.

"In fact," I said, "it's only been within the last

two years that she quit seeing her. I think they keep in touch though. I've heard so much about her, I feel as if I know her myself."

"You ever been to a shrink?" he asked, his mouth full. It amused me that he felt so comfortable asking such a personal question, but then I felt totally comfortable answering. I'd come, supposedly, to discuss blackmail, and instead we were sipping chilled wine on the deck overlooking the lake, feasting on gourmet delicacies. Only in Cedar Hills, I thought, smiling.

"Martha was really persistent about getting me to see someone after my first lover died, but I just didn't feel like talking about it. Diane and I had been dealing with the dying process for so long together, and then when she finally did die, it was almost a relief. I know that sounds terrible, but I was just so exhausted and so depleted, I almost wished I'd been able to go with her. I wasn't suicidal or anything. I was just tired. The thought of trudging through the whole thing with a stranger seemed more than I could fathom. I moved up here to get away from the memories. To start over. It's not that I don't believe in the value of therapy, I just knew that for me, at that time in my life, I wasn't ready for it. It's funny, though. Now that I can talk about it, I don't need to as much."

I looked up and was surprised to see tears in Rick's eyes. Worse, I felt them spring up in my own. I hadn't cried over Diane in ages, and now with this perfect stranger, I felt myself ready to lose it. I looked out at the lake, willing myself to stuff the unwanted emotion back down where it came from.

Rick put his hand over mine, and we sat there like that for some time, holding hands, thinking our own sad thoughts in silence.

"Thanks," I said, at last, pulling my hand back and reaching for my glass.

"Hey, what are friends for?" he asked, smiling. And I knew he meant it. At that moment I knew that no matter how this case turned out, I had already come out ahead. And suddenly, I had a fierce desire to figure out who was intruding on these gentle people's lives.

"Tell me about your neighbors," I said, reaching for my note pad. He sighed, as if the thought of getting down to business were distressing.

"We hardly know them," he admitted. "There's an older lady, Mrs. Krause, who drives a yellow boat. She lives in the house just north of us. She's all alone, except when her relatives visit. Then there's all sorts of partying going on. The grandkids water ski. But the rest of the time, we hardly ever see her. The house next up from her used to belong to a family from Eugene, but they sold it, and no one's moved in yet. The only other house on that side belonged to an older couple, but the guy died not very long ago and his wife sold the place. Then, south of us is only one house, and it's been vacant for as long as we've been here. I don't know who owns it. That's it for the neighbors. Like I said, it's hard to believe we've offended anyone. There's hardly anyone around to offend."

I handed Rick the estimate I'd drawn up the night before and he looked it over briefly, nodding without comment.

"I guess I'll start with the lady next door," I said,

pushing back my chair. "While I'm gone, why don't you go down to my boat and see who I brought for a visit? They're either curled up in a patch of sun in the boat or they're tearing up your dock by now."

"You brought your cats?" he asked, eyes wide. "In the boat?"

"Oh, they love it," I said. "I should be back in less than an hour."

I left him to clean up and let myself out. It felt good to move around and I enjoyed the short walk to the neighbor's house. I'd seen a yellow boat docked in front, so I was pretty sure Mrs. Krause was home. The place was kept up nicely, with well-tended flower pots on the porch and a fresh paint job on the house. When I rang the door bell, a very tentative, nervous-sounding voice answered through the closed door. I imagined she didn't have many callers.

"Mrs. Krause? I'm Cassidy James, a private investigator." I held up my license for her to see through the peephole in the door.

The door flew open so quickly I jumped back, startled. In her late sixties, Mrs. Krause was a pleasantly plump woman, with orangish hair that clearly came from a bottle. Despite the dubious color, it was well coifed, and she was wearing a dress more suitable for going to town than for lounging around the house. All dressed up, I thought, and no place to go.

"Come in, won't you?" she said nervously, ushering me into the hallway. Her house was immaculate, the smell of lemon furniture wax in the air. She led me into a small living room and gestured to a flowery sofa which looked like it had never been sat on. With good reason, I thought, sitting on the

37

stiff, unyielding cushion. I sat up so high, my feet barely touched the floor. Mrs. Krause took a seat across from me, in what was obviously a more comfortable ottoman, and shot me a feeble smile.

"What's this all about?" she asked, turning the band on her ring finger around and around.

"I'm investigating a case involving blackmail and wondered if you might be able to help me." I hadn't planned what to say, but her reaction was so volatile that I felt I'd stumbled onto the blackmailer herself.

"How did you know!" she demanded. Her eyes were wide with fear and something else I couldn't pin down. Guilt? "I haven't told a soul!" she added, eyes darting to the curtained window. Why someone would live on the lake and then close off the view with curtains was beyond me. Was it fear of having someone see in, I wondered, or something else?

"Why don't you tell me about it?" I suggested, not having a clue what she was talking about.

"Do you mind showing me your identification again," she asked. I dug in my pocket for my license and got up to show it to her. She took a long time studying it. Finally she handed it back. "Who sent you here?" she asked, starting to sound paranoid.

"I came on behalf of a client," I said patiently.

"Then your client's the one!" she blurted.

"Which one is that?" I asked, starting to regret this little visit.

"The one who's been blackmailing me!" Her eyes narrowed at me, as if I'd somehow tricked her.

"I think you better start from the beginning," I said. "I'm working for someone else who, I can assure you, is not blackmailing anyone. In fact, he

38

himself is being blackmailed. Under the circumstances, it seems possible your cases might be connected. If I can help you, I will."

"I should've gone to the police," she said, "but I just can't. The whole thing is so personal!" Mrs. Krause stood up and began pacing back and forth as she talked. "A few weeks ago, I received a threat in the mail. They said they knew my little secret and that they'd tell my son if I didn't cooperate with them. That was it. Two days later I got another one. This time they gave specific details about my so-called secret, proving they knew something. They said if I didn't leave town for good, they'd expose everything to my family. Then I started getting the calls." Her voice wavered, and she looked close to panic.

"Did they ask for money?" I asked, beginning to wonder if some new developers had their eye on Cedar Ridge. Lately, condos had begun to spring up all along the coast. It was only a matter of time before they discovered Rainbow Lake.

"No. Just for me to pack up and leave. The calls are the worst. This creepy voice saying 'Time's running out, Hazel. Are your bags packed yet? I have your son's phone number in my hand. Maybe I'll give him a call now!' " The fear in her eyes was vivid.

"What did you say?" I asked.

"I just kept asking who he was, how he knew these things, what he wanted. And he kept repeating that if I didn't leave town, he'd ruin me." It was difficult to imagine this woman having the kind of secret that could destroy anyone.

"Do you have the letters?" I asked. She nodded and went to retrieve them. On both envelopes was the scrawled word "Bitch." The letters were created with a word processor, like those sent to Rick and Towne.

"Do you have any idea why someone would want you to leave the area?" I asked.

"I haven't the vaguest notion. I hardly know my neighbors. I was friendly with the couple two houses up, the Jacobs, but when Harry passed away so suddenly, Agnes just sold the place. Took the first offer she got and moved back to the city. There's a couple of fellas who live next door. I've waved to them a few times but they keep pretty much to themselves. And the Bakers, who used to live right next door on this side, sold their house last month and no one's moved in yet." She was talking rapidly, pacing as she spoke. Suddenly, her eyes narrowed and she looked directly at me. "You said someone else is being blackmailed too. Is it by the same person who's doing this to me?"

"I'm bound to my clients' confidentiality, so I can't give you any specifics," I said, "but yes, I think there's a good chance you're both being blackmailed by the same party."

"Can you find out who?" she asked, coming back to sit across from me. For the first time, I saw a glimmer of hope in her eyes.

"Well, I'm sure going to try. It might be helpful if I knew a little more about your situation, though. Can you tell me what it is exactly that the blackmailer is threatening to expose?" The hope was extinguished as quickly as it had popped up, replaced with utter dread. I let the silence hang between us, giving her time to think it over. When she finally spoke, her voice was small and tight.

"Nobody, I mean absolutely nobody knows about this. And it's nobody's damn business either." Beneath the fear was barely controlled fury.

"Anything you say to me will be held in the strictest confidence." I gave her my most trustworthy look. She waved me off.

"Oh, it's not you I'm worried about. I can't figure out how anyone else could know. I never even told my husband!" And then, with a strange mixture of anguish and relief, she told her story.

Hazel Krause had been married for five years when at last she'd gotten pregnant. Elated, she'd done everything her doctors had told her, and her husband who was stationed in Guam at the time had arranged for a full month's leave to coincide with her delivery. But two months early, Hazel had gone into premature labor and after nearly twenty hours of extreme agony, the doctors finally performed an emergency Caesarian. The baby was stillborn, and worse, Hazel Krause was irreparably damaged. The doctor informed her that she would never be able to have children.

At the same time, in the same hospital, a teenager named Sage Winter gave birth to a healthy baby boy. Sage was fourteen. The father of the baby was thirteen. And Sage had been put in the same room as Mrs. Krause. It had been a no-brainer, in retrospect. Sage's father, a prominent businessman, had taken care of everything. And several days later when both women were released, Hazel Krause had a fine-looking baby boy named Thomas Krause.

Of course, it hadn't been legal. Hazel had never told her husband. She'd never told anyone. And until last month when she'd received a letter from a Sage

Cannon in Seattle, she had simply put the matter out of her mind. Tommy was her son, and that was that. The letter from Sage had knocked the breath right out of her. But Sage had been adamant. She did not want to disrupt their lives. She did not want to see her son. She simply wanted to express a very long overdue thank you. She went on to tell Hazel about her current life, her family — she had three grown children of her own — and her success as a real estate agent. The letter had put to rest any lingering fear in Hazel's mind that someday a woman would appear out of nowhere to reclaim her natural son.

And then, two weeks later, she'd received the threat.

"Kind of coincidental, don't you think?" I asked. "You don't hear anything for all these years and then wham, within a few weeks you get two different letters?"

"I know. It's the first thing I thought of. But it doesn't make any sense. Except for Sage and her father, no one knew about the 'adoption.' In her letter, Sage talked about having kept the secret all these years. If she didn't tell, and I didn't tell, then how did anyone find out?"

"What about hospital records? Surely, the nurses and doctor knew about the switch."

Hazel shook her head vehemently. "The nurse that helped us change the papers was over sixty. I read her obituary seven years ago. The doctor never knew one thing about it."

"Maybe after Sage wrote you the letter, she told someone and they in turn told someone else," I said, thinking it sounded pretty far-fetched.

"But they're not asking for anything!" she cried.

"All they want is for me to leave town. Why would someone up in Seattle care about my leaving Cedar Hills?"

Good point, I thought. I didn't think the blackmailers, whoever they were, lived in Seattle. I thought they were right here in Cedar Hills. One of our own friendly neighbors. Someone wanted the only two neighbors left on Cedar Ridge to vacate the premises. It made me wonder about the other recently departed neighbors. Had they also received threats? And if they had, what secrets had the blackmailers threatened to reveal? And more importantly, how was somebody finding out all these secrets? It may not have been difficult to figure out that Rick and Towne were a couple, but Mrs. Krause's secret seemed a bit more complicated.

"Could anyone have seen Sage's letter here at the house? Maybe a housekeeper, or even a burglar?" I asked.

"I burned the letter as soon as I read it," she said, shaking her head. "Maybe someone read it before she sent it, but not once it got to my house. And like I said, if it were someone up there, I think they'd be asking for money, not for me to leave town. It just doesn't make any sense."

"Well, I'll do what I can," I said, pushing myself off of the uncomfortable sofa. I gave her one of my business cards and she walked me to the door.

"I've been a nervous wreck over this," she said. "I was sitting here thinking I should hire someone to look into this, and then as if by magic, there you were. I want to hire you to find the party responsible for this. I know you're already working for someone else, but you said yourself the cases are probably related, and I won't get a moment's rest until this thing is settled. What exactly is your fee?"

When I told her, she went straight to her purse and wrote out a check.

"Uh, I usually just add up the hours, and let people know how much they owe."

"Well, go ahead and keep track of the hours, dear. If you get past that amount, let me know. If you have some left over, consider it a tip. But I want you working full time to catch whoever is doing this to me. Before they make good on their threat."

I made her promise to call me if she heard from the blackmailers again and I headed back to Rick's place, a million ideas fighting for attention.

I should have known better than to leave the cats in Rick's care. They were out on the front deck, Gammon licking what was left of the liver pâté, Panic making short work of the crab. Rick was sitting back in a blue director's chair, sipping wine and laughing.

"Oh, terrific!" I said. "They'll never eat Purina again!" Actually, I'd been looking forward to some more of the pâté myself.

When the cats had finished their snack, Rick and I took them back down to my boat for the ride home. I was trying to figure out how to tell him about Mrs. Krause without breaching confidentiality. It was definitely strange having two different clients for the same case, and I decided I would have to ask Mrs. Krause for permission to discuss her part of the case with Rick and Towne, minus the secret of course, and vice versa. Once they both agreed, it would make everything infinitely easier.

I told Rick I'd be getting back in touch soon and

hopped into my boat, noticing with interest that the house across the lake sat almost directly opposite Rick and Towne's place, and that someone was standing at the window peering down at us. When I reached for the binoculars I kept in the boat, the figure disappeared behind a rapidly closing curtain. Another neighbor worth visiting, I thought. I sped away from the dock, with both cats gripping the bow cushions, their noses pointed directly into the wind.

Chapter Four

When I pulled into my boathouse, I was surprised to see Jess Martin's boat tied up to my dock. He drove a big, clunky fishing boat that he'd won in a poker game several years ago. He'd gotten it running, but no amount of mechanical know-how was ever going to make that boat look good. From the dock, I could see Jess, his hair tied back in a pony tail, pushing a wheelbarrow full of dirt toward the back yard. He and little Jessie had been planning to help me put in a greenhouse before the latest storm, and I guess they'd taken it upon themselves to start without me. I hurried to the backyard and sure enough, they were both hard at work at the far end of the yard.

When she saw me, Jessie came running up to the back porch. Like her dad, she wore her long, golden hair tied back in a pony tail. She was wearing faded jeans and an old pair of red sneakers. Her skinny arms were already sunburned from the shoulders down. She was all arms and legs, with braces on her teeth and wire-rim glasses that made her look like an owl. Hard to picture her holding a big old handgun in both hands and blowing the top of her brother's head off. If I hadn't been there, and seen it myself, I wouldn't have believed it possible. But then, neither her father nor I would likely be alive right now if she hadn't done it.

"Hey, Cassidy. Where've you been? We've got all the post holes dug without you!"

"Looks good," I said, roughing her hair. "You guys look like you could use a break. Coke, iced tea or Gatorade?"

"Tea for me," she said, stamping the dirt off her shoes on the porch step.

"I'd take a beer," Jess said, coming up to stomp his own boots on the porch. I got a couple of beers out of the fridge and poured some iced tea into a large plastic glass for Jessie. The three of us sat on the back deck, admiring the start on the greenhouse, while Gammon and Panic examined the work up close.

It was warm and comfortable, sitting in the afternoon sun, making small talk. Jessie was excited about school almost being out, and she reminded me about ten times that I had promised she could tag along on one of my cases this summer. Jess was cheerful, despite his recent break-up with Lilly. I was trying to think of a graceful way to broach the subject, but Jessie beat me to it.

"Dad and Lilly broke up," she said, matter-of-factly. "She was too moody, huh, Dad?"

"There's more to it than that, Pie Face," he said. Jessie wrinkled her nose at the nickname. At eleven, she was starting push her independence.

"You okay with it?" I asked Jess, tapping his shoulder. Jess wasn't big on affectionate displays, but since the shooting, we'd gotten pretty close. When his wife moved out, he'd been almost relieved. Things had been bad between them for a long time. Even Jessie seemed to be doing pretty well considering all that had happened. I knew she missed her mother, but that didn't stop her from trying to fix her dad up with others. And he hadn't exactly been hurting for female companionship. He was tall and recklessly good-looking, with a perpetual stubble of beard on his face and an easy grin to go with compelling green eyes. He'd been the number one most eligible bachelor in Cedar Hills for less than a year and had already dated most of the available women in town.

"I'm kind of relieved it's over, to tell you the truth," he said. "She was starting to wear on my nerves."

"Mine too," Jessie piped up. "I don't see why you guys can't just get together." She looked pointedly from her dad to me. "That would be perfect."

Jess and I both laughed, but Jessie was watching us intently.

"There's a lot you don't know yet, kiddo," Jess said, tugging gently on her pony tail.

She moved away indignantly. "I know more than you think I do," she said staring out at the garden.

"Oh yeah?" I said, trying to keep it light. "Like what?"

"Like the fact that you and Erica were more than just friends. And that you like girls better than boys. I'm not stupid, you know." This was not the conversation I'd expected, and I found myself at a loss for words.

"Well, then," Jess said, "I guess you do understand why Cassidy and I can't just get together, to use your phrase."

"But it's not fair!" She pouted. "You don't have to, you know, like, have sex or anything. You could just be, like, family."

Despite the awkwardness of the situation, I couldn't help laughing, and neither could Jess. Jessie glared at both of us, looking close to tears.

"We're not laughing at you," I said. "It's just that you're so honest about stuff, and people don't usually talk so candidly about these things. But since you've brought it up, we may as well discuss it. Okay?"

She nodded, biting her lip.

"You're right about my preferring women, Jessie. That's just the way I am. Most people like the opposite sex, but some people are different. And yes, Erica was that way too." Funny, I thought, I'd just used the past tense to talk about Erica.

"And your friend, Martha. The cop," she said, looking at me for confirmation.

"Yes, and Martha too. So you see, no matter how much your dad and I like each other as friends, we will never be more than that."

"But couldn't you change? If you tried?" she

asked. I had to bite my lip to keep from laughing again. The question was in dead earnest.

"I could fake it," I said. " A lot of people do, to be more socially acceptable. But I would never be truly happy. I'd be living a lie. That's not something I'm willing to do, Jessie. I like being who I am."

She seemed to mull this over, sipping her tea thoughtfully. Jess gave me a look over her head, as if to say, "Hey, sorry about this," but I shrugged, letting him know it wasn't his fault. It was bound to come up sooner or later.

"Does it bother you that I'm a lesbian?" I had to ask. Her big green eyes looked huge behind her glasses.

"Why should it bother me?" she asked. "I mean, except for I wish you could be like, you know, my stepmom. But if you mean does it bother me that you're different from me and my dad, I don't see why it should. Should it?"

Now I did laugh. "No, it definitely shouldn't. But some people are prejudiced against people who are different from them. You know, like hating someone for the color of their skin. It's the same kind of thing. There are a lot of people full of hatred in this world, Jess. And some of them hate gays."

"Well, if anyone says anything about you," she said, standing up, "they'll have me to answer to." She strode off the porch, across the back yard, her pony tail bouncing in the breeze, as if she were marching off to war.

"Well, that went pretty smoothly," Jess said, humor in his voice.

"Sure took me by surprise. How long has she known?"

"Beats me," he said. "She's a funny kid, Cass. Her psychologist asked if she could give her an IQ test. Turns out the kid is like, close to genius. Scored in the one-sixties. Doctor Carradine says she should be in special classes. So next year she's going to go to school up in Kings Harbor, instead of here. I haven't discussed it with her yet. I thought maybe I'd wait until the summer. By the way, Doctor Carradine would like to meet with you, if it's okay."

I gave Jess a startled look, and he grinned.

"She won't bite, honest," he said. "She's a real nice lady. I know how you feel about shrinks, Cass, but Doctor Carradine has been real good with Jessie, and she just wants to talk to someone else who was there, uh, when it happened."

Both Jess and Jessie had been seeing Doctor Carradine since the shooting, at Martha's insistence. It seemed the whole world was either seeing or had seen Doctor Carradine. And now it looked like I was finally going to meet the great therapist myself, like it or not.

"When does she want to meet?" I asked, watching Jessie playing with the cats by the stream.

"I'll give you her number. If you call her tomorrow, she can probably set up an appointment before Jessie's next session, next week. Are you sure you don't mind?" he asked, swigging the remains of his beer.

"Hey, for Jessie, I'd even brave the dentist," I said. But in my heart, I felt a strange trepidation. For some reason, shrinks made me nervous.

Chapter Five

Saturday morning I woke early to another sun-
filled day. I sat with my coffee at the kitchen table,
organizing note cards for my investigation. I made a
list of people to call, things to do, places to go. Way
down the list was a reminder to phone Jessie's
therapist. I put it off until last, but by nine o'clock,
I'd done everything else I could think of, so I made
the call. I spoke to a receptionist who said they could
fit me in at five on Monday, right after Doctor
Carradine's last appointment. Terrific, I thought.

Maybe she'd be in a hurry to quit for the day, and it would be over quickly.

I'd spoken to both Mrs. Krause and Rick, and both had happily agreed that I could share their cases with the other, after I assured Mrs. Krause that her secret would not be a part of the discussion.

Next, I'd called the real estate office, hoping to find out who had bought the recently sold houses on Cedar Ridge. Susie Popps, the loquacious agent told me she didn't personally know, but she'd be happy to look into it for me.

"Now, I do know who just bought the very top of Cedar Ridge," she said, her voice overflowing with enthusiasm.

"The top of the ridge?" I asked, surprised. "Who was that?"

"The new minister in town, Reverend Love. They're going to hold some kind of religious retreats up there, from what I understand."

"When did he buy it?"

"Oh, a few months ago. About the time he started preaching at the old Methodist church. Have you heard him yet? He's quite the orator."

"No, I haven't had that pleasure," I said. "Has the ridge been on the market for long? I didn't even know it was for sale."

"Well, it just belonged to the county and it wasn't doing them any good. You can't get to it except by foot, and then it's a pretty long hike. The scouts used to go up there for weekend camp-outs, but other than that, no one's been up there for ages. The forestry service left that one ridge alone back when they clear-cut this whole area on account of there was no way to get the logs back down off the ridge. It's one of the few places left around here with original red cedar. I imagine it'll be a perfect spot for a retreat."

"Yes, I imagine it will," I said. "Listen, Susie, I'd sure appreciate it if you could find out who the new owners of those houses are for me. I'll stop by this afternoon when I'm in town and see what you've got."

"You do that, Cassidy. And say, if you ever want to sell that neat little place of yours out on the lake, I'd sure like first crack at it. The way the prices have sky-rocketed lately, I'm sure you could make a killing." She giggled and hung up before I could answer.

After that, I'd searched the white pages for an Agnes Jacobs, the widow of the recently deceased neighbor on Cedar Ridge. There was an A. Jacobs in Kings Harbor, who turned out to be Arthur, and that was it. As a last-minute thought, I checked under Harry Jacobs, and sure enough, there he was in Riverton, just fifteen miles north of Cedar Hills. Poor Agnes, still using her husband's name, even after he'd died. I copied down the number and address, deciding I'd probably get more information in person than over the phone. So after making the appointment with Doctor Carradine, I bundled up my house trash, bid my kitties *adieu,* and hopped in my Sea Swirl for a quick trip over to the marina.

Tommy was at it again, tossing his spinner right into the mouth of the creek, reeling in lazily, not a care in the world. When he heard the boat motor, he jumped up, threw the rod down on the dock and pretended to examine a hole in the dock with

54

fascination. I grinned at him and waved my finger back and forth. Even from a distance, I could see his face redden. Busted twice in two days. Tommy was flirting with danger.

I tossed my trash bags into the marina dumpster and climbed into my black Jeep Cherokee, letting the engine warm up before heading north. It was a short but picturesque drive, with sand dunes on the left arching gracefully toward the ocean a mile away while towering trees lined the curvy road on the right allowing occasional glimpses of glistening lakes and streams. The road was blessedly uncrowded this time of year.

Riverton is a quaint little town, right on Highway One. Motels and diners dot the roadside, catering to the logging truckers and tourists passing through. A half-mile out of town, the charter fishing boats do a booming business during salmon season, and along the Salmon River there are hordes of boat rentals, tackle shops and riverside cafes.

The houses in Riverton are divided into three sections — those along the river, those overlooking the harbor and those within walking distance to town. I took out my map and searched for Pelican Lane, finally finding it down by the harbor. The Jacobs had lived in a house overlooking Rainbow Lake, and it made sense that Mrs. Jacobs would choose another house with a view. So I was surprised when I pulled up to an older, clapboard house, three streets back from the water, on a plain residential street. There was a white Buick in the driveway and the front door was open. I assumed Mrs. Jacobs was home.

I rang the doorbell and stepped back away from the closed screen. A ferocious yipping ensued, and I could see an apricot toy poodle racing back and forth on the hardwood entryway, eager to nip at my ankles.

"Yes? Can I help you?" a melodious voice inquired. She was wearing gray corduroy pants and a pink sweater, sleeves pushed up to the elbows. Her hair was wrapped in a pink scarf, and her face, creased with wrinkles, was generously dotted with age spots. If she was a day, she was eighty, but her blue eyes were alert and filled with child-like wonder.

"I'm Cassidy James, a private investigator from Cedar Hills," I said, smiling at her through the screen while holding up my I.D. "Are you Agnes Jacobs?"

"Yes, I am," she said. "Paprika, stop that! Won't you come in? She won't bite," she said, as I edged past the yipping poodle. "Well, she might if she could, but all her front teeth have fallen out, poor thing." Her voice had a sing-song quality. I followed her into a comfortably furnished living room and took a chair across from her. Paprika came over and sniffed excitedly at my feet, apparently deciding that I was a cat person, before running stiff-legged back to Agnes. She picked up the little dog and petted her while we spoke.

"You used to live on Cedar Ridge," I said getting right to the point. "Is that right?"

"Oh, my yes. Years and years we had that place. But then Harry passed on a few months ago, and I decided it was time to move into town. Do you mind my asking what this is all about?"

I told her briefly about the blackmailing going on

with some of the people on the ridge, and her eyes grew wide.

"Letters or calls?" she asked.

"Actually, both," I said, curious. "Why do you ask?"

"Because just before his heart attack, Harry had received some disturbing calls. He wouldn't tell me what they were about, but they clearly upset him. And then, the day he died, he received a letter in the mail. It was right there on the dock, reading that letter, that he suffered the attack. It was still in his hand when he fell. I saw him go down and I called nine-one-one, and then I rushed down to the dock. Well, I don't move as fast as I used to, but I can tell you I fairly flew down those steps. Still, by the time I got there, he was already gone." Tears had gathered in her bright eyes, but her voice was strong and steady. "He was an old man, Harry was. Would have been eighty-five next month. But he wasn't in bad health at all. Never had a lick of heart problems, as far as we knew. And then, just like that," she snapped her fingers, "he was gone. I can tell you, I never knew the days could be so long. When you spend your whole life with someone, and then they up and leave you, well it kind of takes the wind out of your sails. But you didn't come to listen to an old, lonely woman prattle on, did you? How can I help?"

"Mrs. Jacobs, did you read that letter? It might be important." I mentally crossed my fingers.

"Agnes, please. And, yes, eventually, of course, I did look at it. I gathered it with the other mail and just laid it on the table. It wasn't until several days later that I thought to look at it. I can tell you, it was a shock! Such vile language! But I had no idea who had sent it, or what it was about. Apparently someone thought Harry had a secret, and they threatened to expose it if he didn't move away.

"Well, I knew everything there was to know about Harry Jacobs, and I couldn't think of one thing he'd ever done that someone could blackmail him with. But the letter said they'd tell his wife the whole story if he didn't leave. I couldn't imagine what whole story they could be talking about, but of course, that was the point, wasn't it? Obviously, there was something about Harry I didn't know. Something terrible enough that the threat of exposure sent him literally to his death. I don't know what the secret was, and I don't ever want to know. I just hope that whoever wrote that letter rots in hell."

The little dog had grown agitated as Agnes spoke, and she plunked him down on the carpet.

"Do you still have the letter?" I asked, hoping against hope.

"Burned it on sight," she said, daring me with her eyes to challenge this decision. I didn't.

"It must be very hard on you," I said. "Losing your husband and then having to go through the whole ordeal of moving. How soon after he died were you able to sell the house?"

"Well, now. That was the funny part. Sometimes I think the Lord is watching out for us after all. You see, the day after the funeral, there was a card tacked to our door, asking if we were interested in selling. I called the number and the man made an offer, and that was that. It was a fair offer and he took care of all the closing costs. In fact, when he learned why I was so anxious to sell, that my husband had just passed away, he even helped arrange for the movers to pack me up and get me settled in here. Of course, this is just a rental. I've got myself on a waiting list to get into the Palisades Retirement Inn, over on the river. I'm not ready for the old folks home yet, but it would be nice to be around some people my own age."

I stayed and chatted with Agnes Jacobs for some time, even though I knew she had nothing more to add. She was an engaging woman, full of witty insights and colorful stories. When I finally took my leave, I gave her my card and told her to give me a call when she got ready to move, that I'd be glad to give her a hand with the heavy stuff. And even though I'd stayed, sitting idly as if I hadn't a care in the world, inside my stomach was doing little flip flops of excitement. When I'd asked her the name of the man who'd bought her place, and who'd been so helpful in arranging her quick departure from Cedar Ridge, she'd told me it was the new minister in town, Reverend Love.

Chapter Six

Susie Popps bounced out of the alcove she used for an office and waved a handful of papers. "I've got it right here," she said. "And you'll never guess what!" She led me into a corner where two chairs were pulled up to a metal desk, and plunked down in one of them. I took the other.

"All three houses have been bought by the same company. I've never heard of them and have no idea what they do, but it's not unusual for a company or corporation to buy a lakefront property to use for business retreats and such. But to buy three on the same stretch does seem unusual."

"What's the name of the company?" I asked.

"Loveland Incorporated."

I'd been waiting to hear Reverend Love's name again and was disappointed when she had said it was a company. Now my hopes rose again. Reverend Love had bought the top of Cedar Ridge. Reverend Love had personally arranged to quickly move Agnes Jacobs out of her house, buying it just days after her husband had died, conveniently being in the right place at the right time. Reverend Love was no doubt connected to Loveland Inc., and most likely the author of some pretty nasty blackmail notes as well. Thinking it, though, was one thing. Proving it was something else entirely.

The old Methodist church was on the outskirts of town, about two blocks from the real estate agency. I decided that since I was in the neighborhood and all, I'd just stop in. It was a small, rectangular building with peeling white paint and an old marquee that bore the cryptic message, "Come march with the army of Love." I'd noticed the message over a month ago, but hadn't given it much thought. New ministers came and went in Cedar Hills fairly regularly. So far, I'd managed to avoid them all.

The front doors were locked, so I peeked through the windows as I edged around to the back. The place was empty. It was not a building that would inspire many, I thought. A large, wooden Jesus lay impaled above the wood pulpit. The pews, also wood, looked ancient, and even from the window I could imagine splintered derrieres and slivered thighs. I

61

pushed my way between two blue-budded hydrangea bushes and found what I'd been looking for, a back door. It too was locked.

The one real valuable skill my mentor Jake Parcell had taught me was lock-picking. Upon completion of my internship, he had given me my very own set of picks, and I'd been dying for a chance to use them. Unfortunately, they were at home, so I had to improvise.

After screwing around for a while with a paperclip from my pocket, to no avail, I stepped back, looked in both directions and gave one mighty kick. The door swung open with ease, and I was so pleased with myself that it took a minute to realize the room wasn't empty. Sitting behind an old wooden school teacher's desk was a pint-sized man with red wavy hair and a shocking array of freckles splashed across his face. More shocking though, was the pistol in his hand. It was aimed at me.

"Uh, sorry," I said lamely, backing up. "Didn't know anyone was home."

"And you are?" he asked, his nasal tone imperious.

I would have lied, if I could have thought quickly enough, but my brain seemed to have taken a hasty vacation.

"Cassidy James, private investigator," I said, slowly removing my license from my pocket and holding it up for him to see. As if that made any difference, I thought. "I'm looking for Reverend Love."

"Did it not occur to you to knock?" he said, his voice both whiny and dictatorial. He lowered the gun but did not, I noticed, put it away. He set it on the desk, next to the IBM computer he'd been working at, keeping a firm grip on the handle.

"It's a bad habit," I said. "I'm not used to people locking their doors around here. I just wanted to leave the Reverend a quick note. Do you know where I might find him?" I was betting this officious ninny wasn't the Reverend. If he was, I was in deep doodoo. I wasn't prepared to confront the Reverend just yet.

"He's out," he said. "Perhaps I could give him a message?"

"Perhaps you could," I said. "And who, may I ask, are you?" He pursed his lips, weighing whatever pros and cons there might be in revealing this sacred information. Finally, the pros must have won out, because he swiveled around in his wooden teacher's chair and stood up.

"I am the Reverend's accountant," he said. "Herman Hugh Pittman." I half-expected him to say, "The Third." Anyone sadistic enough to name a kid Herman Hugh probably came from a long line of them.

"Well, it's certainly been a pleasure chatting with you, Herman Hugh," I said, easing out the door. "And sorry if I startled you. If I'd known you were here, I would have knocked." I hoped the illogic of this would confuse him long enough for me to scoot out, but the little weasel was having none of it.

"What message did you wish me to convey to the Reverend?" he asked, inching toward me. He was just a wisp of a man, but even so, his light blue eyes seemed menacing.

"Tell him to expect a large crowd tomorrow in church," I improvised. "He might want to set up some extra chairs. I hear there's a lot of folks headed this way."

I smiled my most innocent smile, and waved good-bye. His eyes had narrowed and then grown quite large at this message. I left him wondering whether I was indeed friend or foe. But there was no doubt in my mind. Herman Hugh and I were never going to be friends.

Chapter Seven

I'd spent the remainder of that Saturday afternoon thinking up ways to prove my suspicions about the good Reverend, and largely drawing blanks. Now, I was sitting in Martha's apartment, looking out the huge bay window overlooking Kings Harbor. Not the town, the actual harbor. Tug boats and fishing boats bobbed on the choppy water while pelicans and gulls put on an aerial display. She brought me a glass of wine and settled down on the sofa next to Tina, slipping her arm around Tina's shoulders. They looked good together, I thought for the hundredth time. Martha's creamy white against Tina's coffee brown. They were both dressed up, and unless I was imagining it, Martha had even put a little blush on her cheeks. There was no denying it, Martha was smitten.

I'd been telling them about my investigation, right up to my barging in on Herman Hugh.

"Seems kind of funny that a Reverend's accountant would carry a gun," Tina said, frowning.

"Seems kind of funny that a preacher in these parts would even need an accountant," Martha added, sipping her wine.

"That's kind of what I thought," I said. "If he's raking in the bucks, he's sure not spending any of it sprucing up the church. It looks worse than when the Methodists ran it."

"What religion is he preaching, anyway?" Tina asked. She leaned forward and took a cracker with cheese and fed it to Martha. She was incredibly sexy, I thought. Tall and sensuous, her moves were graceful and fluid. By far, she was Martha's best find. I only hoped it would last. So far, the relationship had already broken Martha's previous record of nine months. Who knew? Maybe Martha, famous lesbian Don Juan, was settling down at last.

"No one seems to be sure," I said. "The marquee outside says something about marching with the army of Love. Doesn't sound too biblical to me, but it just might fly in Cedar Hills. As a matter of fact, I'm planning on attending tomorrow's service myself. Get a look at the good Reverend."

"Let me see what I can find out about Loveland for you," Martha said. "I won't get to it until Monday, though." She looked lovingly at Tina, and they leaned toward each other to kiss. It was nice to see. Except it made me think of Erica, which in turn did things to my own body that still embarrassed me. And which in turn made me sad. I hadn't heard from Erica, the shithead, for three weeks. I could call her, of course, but for some reason that never seemed to work out. She was always on her way out the door, or just stepping out of the shower, or asleep, or something. It was better if she called me. But I didn't really like playing the role of the little lady waiting at home by the phone. In fact, when I thought about it, Erica was starting to tick me off. Still, I remembered what it was like to kiss her, to touch her satiny skin, and all my anger flew right out the door.

Luckily, I was saved from further torture by the doorbell. My non-date had arrived.

Martha brought Cindy in and introduced us. She was pretty and perky and definitely not my type. Which was fine, apparently with Cindy, who mentioned her lover Roberta about every five seconds. Evidently, this one time, Martha had actually told the truth. She was not trying to set me up. She just needed someone to use the dinner dance ticket. For some reason I couldn't explain, this depressed me.

The four of us climbed into Martha's Ford Explorer and we listened to Cindy chatter nonstop all the way to the Harbor View Lodge, which was conveniently tucked away on the outskirts of town. Kings Harbor is a relatively conservative town, famous for its mill, a myrtle wood factory and its fishing industry. Probably not the kind of place you'd expect to find a couple of hundred lesbians gathered for a dance. But the lodge was far enough away from town that I doubted anyone in the mainstream even knew the event was being held.

There was a line outside. Teenyboppers to octogenarians in every mode of attire stood in twos and threes, alone and in clusters, tickets in hand, waiting to move forward toward the door.

"All these women are lesbians?" I asked, looking around in awe. "In Kings Harbor?"

Martha laughed and squeezed Tina's hand as we joined the throng. "They're all lesbians, but not all from Kings Harbor. Women On Top sponsors a monthly dinner dance, and each month it's in a different city. Last month was Eugene. Before that, it was in Ashland. A lot of people travel to all of them, sort of a monthly vacation. Others just go to the ones close by. But it's a great way to meet new people. What do you think?"

I was still marveling at the sheer number of women. In skirts, pantsuits, jeans, high heels, tennis shoes, shaved heads, curls, you name it, they were there. The thing that really impressed me was how many of the women I found attractive.

The line moved quickly, and before we knew it, we were inside a huge banquet room. It was an impressive crowd.

"Are there always this many people?" I shouted at Martha. The band was already in full swing.

"Not always. The weather dictates a lot of it. Stick with me."

She led the three of us through the throng, weaving in and out like a true veteran. I was actually afraid we'd lose her, and at one point Cindy grabbed my hand for guidance.

At last, Martha managed to find an empty table,

and practically threw herself into a chair, raising her arms wide in victory.

"Actually," Martha admitted, "this is the most crowded I've ever seen it. Must be the sudden good weather." Martha seemed to take in every woman in the room, and I noticed Tina slip her hand beneath the table. Suddenly, Martha's gaze was riveted back on Tina, and I had to stifle a laugh. By God, Martha Harper, I thought, I believe you've finally met your match.

"How do you get a drink?" Cindy asked, looking around. Frankly, I'd been wondering the same thing.

"Well, usually there are waitresses. I'm sure one will be by soon. Or you can always walk up to the bar," Martha said. She pointed to the far wall where dozens of women jostled for position at the bar. Cindy had started to chat again, and I volunteered to go get drinks.

"Tell you what," I said to Martha. "You all sit here and when the waitress comes, order me some Chardonnay. In the mean time, I'll go to the bar and get us a round. Whoever gets the drinks first gets a free round."

Martha's eyes twinkled. She was a betting fool. Before I was even out of my chair, she was signaling madly to one of the waitresses across the room.

The bar was L-shaped, cheap particle board with a fake walnut veneer. Behind the bar were a half dozen women rushing to fill orders, hardly taking time to flirt. There seemed to be six or seven different lines. I chose what looked like the shortest and then chastised myself when all the other lines seemed to move ahead more quickly. I could just picture Martha sipping away at my wine.

Behind me, there was a commotion, and I could hear someone falling into someone else, who in turn fell into me. Before I could right myself, I was shoved into the woman in front of me. I didn't hit her that hard, but it knocked us both off balance.

"I'm really sorry," I said to her back. "Are you okay?"

She turned around, her large green eyes smiling with humor. "This reminds me of a fraternity party," she said, pushing dark curly hair off her forehead. "I only went to one, but it was more than enough. At least no one has challenged me to a chugalug yet."

I found myself enjoying this brief, refreshing encounter. "I take it you don't come to a lot of these," I said, straightening my own hair.

"My first one," she said, edging one notch closer to the bar. "I'm afraid I'm the victim of a good friend's insistence that I finally let my hair down."

"Not you too," I said, laughing. "I've been hounded so long, I finally caved in. But I have to admit, it's a lot different than I thought." She was facing me now, and when the line moved forward, I touched her gently on the arm to let her know to back up.

"Me too," she said, "The last time I went to a gay bar, they were playing disco. Don't tell anyone, but I secretly liked disco."

"I hear it's making a comeback. Though it sounds like you're in for a healthy dose of pure country tonight."

She was in her early forties, I was pretty sure. She had a well-worn look about her, as if she'd been through some things and survived them. She was damned attractive, I thought. Her skin was brown from the sun, which was hard to accomplish in Oregon. She probably took advantage of the outdoors, I mused, noticing the striking contrast of her white teeth against her tan when she smiled. And her eyes were a deep, sea-water green. I realized I was staring at her and felt a blush spread across my cheeks.

"Tell you what," I said. "If the band switches from country to disco, I'll come find you. Show you my best John Travolta impression."

"You do that," she said, holding my gaze before turning to face the bartender. I stood, practically touching her backside while she waited for her drink. I could think of absolutely nothing more to say to her, but I didn't want the conversation to end. When her wine finally came, she turned and we found ourselves face to face, inches apart.

Her green eyes locked with mine, and I felt a tugging deep in my center. People in line were starting to grumble and the person behind me nudged me ever so slightly.

"Maybe I'll see you later?" she said, her own cheeks seeming to blush.

"I hope so." My voice sounded croaky, even to me. God knows what I ordered. By the time I got back to our table, the first round had not only arrived, but was nearly gone. All I could think of, though, was the dark-haired woman with the sexy green eyes and easy smile. I found myself peering over shoulders, straining for a glimpse of her.

"A penny for your thoughts," Martha said, sipping her wine. A guilty blush washed over me and Martha laughed.

"Oh ho!" she said. "I recognize that look. Don't tell me. You met someone."

"Oh, Martha," I said, rolling my eyes. Even I knew I wasn't very convincing.

"Well, where is she?" she persisted.

"She's a figment of your imagination," I said. Or mine, I thought. But I refused to look around again, lest Martha catch me in the act.

Dinner turned out to be an hors d'oeuvres buffet which was actually pretty good. Despite the crowd, there was plenty for everyone. By the time we had finished eating, they were announcing what they called the ultimate country line dance. The woman at the microphone was enthusiastic about it, but the directions seemed impossibly tricky. Martha said to trust her, it would work, and it did sound kind of fun. Everyone was getting into the act, lining up in two rows facing each other.

"You start by dancing with the person across from you," Martha explained as we joined the lines. "Then you switch places, dance with the person kitty-corner to the left, switch places, dance with the person kitty-corner to the right, switch places, and then the person across from you again. That way, your partner always changes, and when the deejay says to slide three paces to the right or left, that mixes it up even more."

I looked at Martha as if she'd just spoken Swahili, but Tina gave me an encouraging wink, and even Cindy seemed game. The idea that I wouldn't be trapped with Cindy as a partner all night cheered me, so I joined the others in one of the lines and waited for the deejay to get started.

The music was definitely country, but it was upbeat and kind of catchy. The deejay led us through the first steps, everyone laughing at her own mistakes. I stepped on my first partner's toes, and my second partner belted me in the chops, but after that we settled down and got into it. I'm a fair dancer, when I'm not nervous or self-conscious. I'm usually at my best after several glasses of wine. By the time we'd made it through the first lick, as the deejay called it, I was kicking up my heels and having a seriously good time.

The women I took so briefly in my arms were as different from one another as I could imagine. One minute I was being led by a silver-haired seventy-year-old who could dance circles around me, and the next I was leading a tentative woman in her twenties who seemed to have at least three feet, all of them lefties. The best dancer by far was an overweight blonde whose eyes were alive with the sheer joy of dancing. She laughed as she twirled me, perspiration soaking her bangs. I was sorry to see her go. I was really into the dance when I looked up to see the dark-haired, green-eyed woman standing across from me. The pit of my stomach dropped suddenly, and I felt my feet grow leaden.

Everyone else around us started and she held her hands out, smiling. My brain had completely stalled on me, but somehow my feet responded. I slid into her embrace as easily as if we were ice-skating partners, my gaze locked with hers as we twirled each other around, using the same steps we'd been using with all of the other partners, but somehow making them different with each other.

She said something into my ear and I caught the word *disco,* but the music was too loud to make out the rest. But the feel of her lips brushing so close to my ear, the feel of her warm breath on my neck, sent shivers down to my toes. Before I could ask her to repeat what she'd said, it was time to switch partners again. Our eyes had scarcely left each other while we danced, and now as we turned our bodies to face our new partners, we continued to hold the gaze. Neither of us smiled at all. It had, in the course of that one brief dance, turned serious.

By the time the dance ended, she was nowhere in sight. I pushed my way through the crowd, craning my neck to find a glimpse of her, but there were just too many women. Instead, Martha found me, her arm protectively around Tina, with Cindy in tow.

"I promised Roberta I'd have Cindy back before midnight," she said. Her look told me it was Martha who was anxious to get Tina back before midnight. I gave one last hurried glance around, but there was no sight of the curly-haired woman with the dark skin and green eyes.

I kicked myself for not getting her name. There were women from all over the state there, and without her name, the chances of my seeing her again were pretty remote. But it had happened so fast, I told myself. And I hadn't expected to meet someone that interested me so much. Not since Erica had I felt such sudden and intense desire. With a pang of guilt, I realized that I hadn't thought of Erica Trinidad once all evening.

"Cat's sure got your tongue," Martha said, using up her monthly quota for clichés as we pulled into her driveway. "Was she at least cute?"

I laughed at her persistence. "Yes," I said. "Yes, she was."

"Did you get her number?" Martha asked, walking me to my Cherokee. I shouted my good-byes to Tina and Cindy who were both rushing inside to use the facilities.

"I only wish I'd thought of it." I leaned to kiss Martha's cheek. "I had a good time, Martha. Thanks."

"Well, you can't hibernate forever, waiting for the gorgeous Ms. Trinidad to remember you exist. It's high time you gave the rest of the lesbian population a chance." She touched my cheek, her big brown eyes giving me her best big-sister stare that told me she'd never let anything bad happen to me. I squeezed her hand, letting her know it was a mutual sentiment, and eased out of her driveway, back to my home on the lake.

That night, after replaying my interactions with the woman a hundred times, a strange thing happened. I began to mentally mix those sea-green eyes with Erica's piercing blue ones. Erica's face became superimposed on the curly-haired woman's, so that by the time I crawled into bed, I could no longer picture either of them clearly. The harder I tried, the worse the problem became, and I fell asleep, mentally kissing a woman who was neither one of them, but both of them wrapped up together.

Chapter Eight

Sunday morning was overcast, and the lake was calm and smooth. I breakfasted on smoked salmon, cream cheese and fresh dill, which I spread liberally on a toasted bagel. I had orange juice and coffee, while the cats waited patiently for me to drop a smidgen of salmon on the floor. This was a game we played. I never came right out and fed them people food. Instead, I pretended to accidentally drop some from the table. I think they knew I did it intentionally, but they liked the game as much as I did.

They were lapping up the last of the salmon while I made notes on my investigation.

Sometime during the night, my dreams had turned from a rather lusty romp with two other women, in which I was the star recipient of repeated and earth-shattering orgasms, to a more mundane scene in which a red-headed weasel of a man aimed a gun at me and called me a booger. I woke up laughing, and it was then, in the still hours of the pre-dawn that I began to fathom the motives behind Reverend Love's blackmail scheme. I'd decided that he was the culprit, and I had a pretty good idea what was driving him to commit these crimes. So I sat at my table sipping coffee, drawing up a plan. When I looked at my watch, it was nearly ten, and if I didn't hurry, I'd be late for the Sunday service.

The crowd milling outside the church reminded me of the women's dance the night before. But what a difference! Cedar Hills's rather diverse collection of characters had arrived en masse, spiffed up in their Sunday finery, seeming to enjoy what I assumed was for most of them a rare church outing. My daily walks had taken me by the church on many a Sunday morning and I'd never seen more than a dozen people lined up at the door. If it hadn't been for Booker telling me about Buddy's new girlfriend, I'd have thought Reverend Love had managed to convert the whole town in the few months he'd been here. But looking around at the milling crowd, I suspected most of them had come because of Buddy.

Gus Townsend was there, with his wife and three kids, looking miserable in a tie and tight-fitting jacket. His eyes were shot with red, and I imagined he'd spent most of the evening at Logger's Tavern, tying one on. Lizzie, who ran the tavern, was also there, looking pretty sharp in a blue blazer and matching slacks. She grinned at me and ambled over.

"Why, Cassidy James! I never expected to see the likes of you in church!" she said, her eyes twinkling, her wide mouth grinning.

"Nor I the likes of you!" I returned. I'd often thought Lizzie would have been better off running a woman's bar, but I was never sure. She kept her personal life extremely private, a nearly impossible task in Cedar Hills, as Rick and Towne had recently discovered.

"You gals here to get your souls saved, or you here like everyone else, to see who Buddy Drake comes in with?" Sheriff Booker asked, joining us on the lawn. He was wearing a string tie, and his cowboy boots were shined to a high polish. As always, his flowing silver hair made him movie-star handsome. Jess Martin saw us and came over, looking somewhat sheepish. He was Buddy's good friend, but even he couldn't resist the temptation of finding out who Buddy's new paramour was. Besides, from the looks of the monetary transactions taking place right under the trees in front of the church, I'd say half the town had a bet on who the lucky lady would turn out to be.

"I just wonder what the new Reverend is going to think when he sees all these people show up," I said. "Does anyone know anything about him?"

Sheriff Booker shot me a quizzical glance, one

eyebrow arching slightly higher than the other, but Lizzie was eager to answer.

"He's a strange duck, if you ask me. Kind of egotistical. Talks as if he's God himself. Makes a big show of liking the little kiddies, but they pull away from him as fast as they can. I've watched him through the window down at the tavern. He hangs out with his little buddy who works across the street at the post office, and he's always lurking around over there, shaking people's hands as they go by, inviting them to church and what not. But like I said, children seem to sense something that we don't, and I'd put my money on a kid's intuition any day." Lizzie usually prided herself on not being a gossip, and I wondered at this sudden change.

Jess was nodding his head, his long pony tail still wet from the shower.

"I'm with you, Lizzie. Something about that guy bugs me. He was in the hardware store the other day, pumping old Joe for information about people on the lake. I was looking for a hacksaw blade, and kinda ducked down so he couldn't see me. He just went on and on, asking all kinds of weird questions that weren't any of his business."

"Like what?" Booker and I asked at the same time.

"Oh, he wanted to know if lots of folks around here owned their own guns, for one thing. He was real interested in people's politics. Were they conservative or liberal, Republican or Democrat. Said he himself was an Independent. Said he didn't trust the government, that it was run by the Jews to placate the niggers. He actually said that. He didn't sound all that much like a minister to me." Jess paused long enough to light a cigarette before going on. "Old Joe was kind of agreeing with him, and that seemed to spur him on. He seemed to like the sound of his own voice, and once he got going, he couldn't stop. But as soon as someone would walk into the store, he'd change the subject, let old Joe wait on them, and then the second they left, he'd start in again. Finally, my legs were starting to cramp from squatting down like that, so I stood up and walked right up to him. You should have seen his face when he saw me. Just for a second, he looked scared, and then he turned all jovial, shaking my hand, inviting me to church, like that. Old Joe was embarrassed as hell. I guess he'd forgotten I was back there. Anyway, the guy's a definite creep."

"Not to mention a bigot," I said.

"Doesn't sound real preacherly to me," Booker added, stroking his mustache thoughtfully. "Anyone actually heard one of his sermons?"

"Ed Beechcomb went last Sunday," Lizzie said. "You could ask him. I think he and Al Morris signed up for one of those all-male retreats." Lizzie rolled her eyes.

"What all-male retreats?" I asked.

"Up there on the ridge, I guess. Sort of a male-consciousness thing. Guys getting in touch with their feelings, or some such nonsense. At least that's what Ed said. Personally, the way he was acting, I wouldn't be surprised if they were really up there watching porno and playing poker all night."

"Well, it oughta be real interesting to see what message he bestows upon us today," Booker said.

People had started filing in, but a lot of us were holding back, waiting to see Buddy Drake arrive.

When the organ started to play and he still hadn't arrived, my group gave him up for a no-show and headed on in. Others just up and left, having no desire to sit through a Sunday sermon. Inside, the place was packed, people craning around every time someone entered. There was so much whispering that it nearly drowned out the music coming from an old pipe organ in the corner. Even Phoebe Stills, the organist, kept looking toward the door while she pounded out a peppy version of "Rock of Ages."

Apparently Herman Hugh had taken my words to heart, because they'd set up extra metal folding chairs in the aisles and along the back. These were already taken, although I noticed that there was still plenty of room in the front pew, where no one seemed to want to sit. We squeezed in behind the folding chairs, the four of us standing with our backs to the wall next to the door.

"That's him!" Lizzie whispered, pinching my arm. "The one who works at the post office!" She pointed to the boy lighting candles beneath the wooden Jesus, and when he turned around, I noticed with a start that it wasn't a boy at all. It was Herman Hugh. He was wearing a white robe, with little tassels around the collar, and his red hair seemed to glow, as if he'd lit himself on fire. The freckles staining his face stood out like angry birthmarks, and even from the back I could see his lips pursed together in a kind of superior smirk. Herman Hugh may have been dressed like an angel, but there was nothing angelic about him.

"What's he do at the post office?" I asked.

"Beats me," Lizzie said. "Been working there ever since John McIntyre quit. He used to help sort and stack, so I guess that's what this one does. I guess he's worked in post offices before, and just happened to be in the right place at the right time. Been there about three months is all."

"About the same time the Reverend Love came to town," I said. And, I thought, about the same time people out on Cedar Ridge started receiving blackmail threats in the mail. Too many instances of being in the right place at the right time for my taste.

The crowd suddenly hushed, and the organ stopped playing. From the left, a tall man in flowing black robes strode into the room. His face was chiseled, with a high protruding forehead, accentuated by his jet black hair which he combed straight back. He had dark, brooding eyes set deep into a pale face, and he wore a pinched, thin smile. Despite myself, a shiver ran right down my spine.

"The Lord has blessed us today." His voice was booming, commanding. "He has brought me to you and now you have come to me. Together we shall join the army of Love and march toward our only salvation."

I looked around the silent room. No one moved. No one scratched their nose, or crossed their legs. The man certainly had presence.

"There are those among you who do not have faith. This I know. Some of you come out of curiosity." He paused, but no one chuckled, though everyone in the room must have been thinking the same thing I was. Lizzie elbowed me gently in the ribs but kept a straight face.

"Some of you come because your wives have urged you to do so. Some come out of a need to be with others, some out of a need to be with God. Some of you doubt there is a God. Some of you have lost faith in your own mankind. Some of you are angry, disgruntled, tired of being pushed around, tired of the government taking more than its share of your earnings. Some of you are mad. And you should be. Some of you will just go on, living each day like meek little lambs, doing what the government tells you to do, following all the rules, getting nowhere. Certainly no closer to heaven on earth. Some of you will resist this message, will close your ears, squeeze your eyes tight, refusing to open up your heart and soul to the message of Love. But some of you, the chosen, the righteous, the courageous, the wise, will join the army of Love, and march with me to salvation. The question you must ask yourself is, which one are you?"

Heads had begun to nod as he spoke, his voice mesmerizing, hypnotic. Jess was scowling, and Booker's eyes had narrowed, so I felt a little better. But there were enough bobbing heads in the crowd to suggest that the Reverend's message, whatever it meant, was having the desired effect.

He was about to go on when the wide doors swung open and in walked Buddy Drake, all five feet of him, decked out in a shiny black suit, white starched shirt and paisley tie. Beside him was a woman of such Titanic proportions that she barely squeezed through the aisle with Buddy beside her. She wore a turquoise chiffon dress that billowed out in great tufts from a truly awesome bosom. I couldn't begin to guess the yardage in that dress. Necks turned, and eyes opened wide with disbelief, delight and wonder. Buddy nodded and smiled, his face aglow as he marched straight down the center aisle, following his yellow-haired, Rubenesque mistress to the front pew, where the two of them sat with great aplomb.

Whispers and cackling filled the room, and quite a bit of money changed hands right there in the church. The Reverend and his cryptic, somewhat menacing sermon had been temporarily forgotten, and when I looked up to see how he was taking being upstaged by Buddy's entrance, the dark look on his face was alarming.

He looked around the room, searching faces, bullying people into silence, but like unruly school kids, most of them paid no attention. His gaze fell on me, and our eyes locked for one terrifying moment. Then he leaned down and said something to Herman Hugh who was seated on the Reverend's right, facing the crowd. Herman Hugh scanned the room until he saw me, and then he whispered something back to the Reverend who nodded and continued staring.

This was going to turn into an old-fashioned stare-down, I thought, and I didn't think I'd come out the victor. Lizzie said something to me and even though it wasn't particularly funny, I laughed aloud and turned as if she and I had been talking all along.

"Let's get out of here," Booker said, moving toward the door. Lizzie and I followed, with Jess bringing up the rear. A good many others had the same idea, and soon the church lawn was filled with nearly as many people as it had been before church started. I could hear the Reverend regain control, his voice stronger and even more commanding than it had been before. "And now we know which of you are indeed the chosen," he boomed. "Thank you, little brother. Your tardy entrance has helped us cull the weak from this, God's army." I could just picture Buddy, nodding happily, so in love he couldn't hear the venom spewing forth.

"The bar doesn't open until noon," Lizzie said. "And it's my day off. But after that performance, I could use a belt or two. Whaddaya say?"

We followed Lizzie to the tavern, just down the street across from the post office. She opened up, turned on the lights which didn't do much to light the place, pulled up all the blinds and went behind the bar. Jess went over and dropped some coins in the juke box, and soon soft rock filled the room. Lizzie poured all four of us a glass of tap beer and refused the sheriff's money when he tried to pay for the round.

"What was that little staring match about?" Lizzie asked, her dark eyes shining.

I glanced up, wondering how much I should say. And suddenly it occurred to me that if I couldn't trust these three, I couldn't trust anyone in Cedar Hills. One way or another, they had become my closest friends, outside of Martha. Booker was my mentor and drinking buddy, Jess was like a brother and Lizzie, if only she'd let her guard down a little, could become a good friend. All of them knew I was gay, and I suspected that the only one bothered was Lizzie. It's what stopped her from getting any closer to me. But it wasn't my sexuality that was irking her, I thought, looking at her. It was hers.

So I told them what I knew.

"You actually kicked the door down, Cassidy?" Booker said, shaking his head, his blue eyes twinkling with delight. "I could arrest you for that."

"What were you hoping to find?" Jess asked, rolling one of his hand-rolled cigarettes.

"I wanted to see if the Reverend had a computer, for one thing. Once I found out he had bought the top of Cedar Ridge, and that Loveland had bought three of the only five houses on Cedar Ridge, I figured it was a good bet he was the one blackmailing the people who own the last two houses. Sure enough, there was a computer in the church office."

"A lot of folks have a computer now days," Booker said.

"But not everyone's got a pistol in the top desk drawer," Lizzie pointed out.

"There's something else," I said. "I can't go into the details, but one of the blackmailing cases really had me baffled until Lizzie mentioned that Herman Hugh works at the post office. See, the blackmailers had information that absolutely no one should have had. One day my client receives a letter which describes a particular incident that only she and the sender know about, and then wham, two weeks later she gets another letter threatening to expose this same information if she doesn't leave town. She couldn't figure out how anyone could have gotten hold of this information. She burned the letter on sight. But what I think is, little Herman Hugh, down there working in the post office, methodically goes through the mail of the people who live on Cedar Ridge. Somehow he reads their mail, reseals it and sends it on. It's through their mail that Herman Hugh and the Reverend discover people's secrets."

Lizzie got up and refilled our glasses. Jess had smoked his cigarette down to his fingers and started to roll another.

"Messin' with the mail is a federal offense," Booker said. "Carries a stiff penalty. I wonder if either of these two jokers has done any time. Think I'll check that out this afternoon."

"But what in the world do they want with Cedar Ridge?" Lizzie asked.

"Ah, therein lies the rub," Booker said, sipping his beer.

"Gotta be the trees," I said, thinking about what Susie Popps had told me. "Cedar Ridge is the only place left with old-growth cedars. I wonder how much each of those trees is worth?"

"Jackson Cromwell just sold off a couple of his acres and got seven hundred dollars for a thousand board feet," Jess said. "That's just one forty-foot tree. Think about it. Some of them trees up on the ridge must be three or four times that big. And there must be hundreds of them. Maybe thousands."

"Plus," Booker added, "I'm sure there's some Douglas fir up there too, which brings in about twelve hundred for a thousand board feet. And I wouldn't be at all surprised if there weren't a few of those Port Orford cedar up there. They're nearly extinct now. They've all been logged. But seeing as how that ridge has never been touched, there's a good chance there might be some still up there."

"What's so special about Port Orford cedar?" I asked. They all turned to look at me like I was an idiot.

"Port Orford Cedar is what the Japanese use to make their temples with," Jess explained. "One log goes for about sixty thousand dollars."

I let the enormity of that sink in.

"No wonder there's none left," I said, finally. "I'm surprised no one has thought to log the ridge before now."

"No way to get the trees down," Booker said. "There's no road access, and it's too tricky to get a helicopter in there. Believe me, if they could've, the logging companies would've been at those trees a long time ago."

"Oh, but there is a road," I said. "It runs right behind the houses on Cedar Ridge. No one uses it, but it's definitely there." There was a long silence as everyone considered this news.

"Well, that's your answer then," Booker said finally. We all looked at him blankly, and he went on. "If a private road which goes through private property has been in use, and goes up to the edge of Mr. X's property, then Mr. X has the right to use the road any time he wants. But if no one has used the road for ten years or more, and it goes through other people's property before it gets to Mr. X's property, then he has to get permission from everyone whose property the road crosses, before he can even step foot on it."

We sat mulling this over in silence.

"So," I said. "If the Reverend bought the top of Cedar Ridge thinking he'd have road access because he knew the road was there, and then found out he couldn't use the road, he might get kind of ticked off."

"And," Lizzie chimed in, "he might decide to buy

up all those little properties himself, just to get the road access he needs to cut down all those trees."

"Except maybe not everyone is real eager to sell," Booker said.

"I wonder if he asked?" I said. "I mean, it seems like it would be easier and cheaper just to offer money to the people who live along the road in exchange for access. Who's going to turn down the new Reverend in town?"

They considered this, sipping their beer in unison.

"Unless for some reason he doesn't want any neighbors," I added.

Booker looked at me strangely. "Which leads the good Reverend to blackmail," he said.

"Yeah," Jess added, swirling the beer in his glass, "and where does a lowly preacher man come up with enough capital to buy up five pieces of lakefront property? Last I heard, they were supposed to live the life of the meek and humble."

Meek and humble didn't exactly describe Reverend Love, I thought, finishing my beer. It was a good question though, and I was eager to find an answer.

Chapter Nine

When people started trickling into the tavern, I took my leave and headed out to Cedar Ridge. Sunday might be a good day to pay a little visit to Rick and Towne's neighbors across the lake, I thought. I pulled up to the dock, an old, weather-beaten rectangle of decaying wood that listed in the water. The stairs leading up to the house were in equal disrepair, and I wondered why no one had fixed the place up. I could tell it had once been a nice house.

It was still overcast, but even so, I was surprised

x

to see the curtains all closed. Most people liked to keep the view to the lake wide open. I knocked on the door, and saw a quick flick of the curtains covering the sliding glass door to my left. Then footsteps, and a tenuous voice.

"Who's there?"

"Cassidy James, private investigator. Can I speak with you for a minute?"

The door opened a crack, and I found myself looking down on a tiny lady, not much over four feet tall. She was wearing a tattered yellow bathrobe and tiny house slippers that had seen better days. Her hair had been brown once but was shot through with gray, and her eyes were watery blue. She was as pale as skim milk.

"Sorry to intrude on you, ma'am. I wondered if I might talk to you and your husband about a case I'm working on." I was trying to peek around her into the room, but she wasn't cooperating. The door wasn't open more than a couple of inches.

"You won't get anything out of him," she said, finally opening the door, "but you can come in if you want to." She turned and shuffled into the living room, leaving me to follow her.

The house was in a shambles, with dirty dishes littering the table tops and general clutter spread throughout. There was the distinct aroma of fried fish, mixed with the pervasive odor of cigarette smoke and something else. It wasn't until I saw her quickly tuck a half-full bottle of scotch behind a sofa cushion that I realized the other smell was stale alcohol.

"Is Mr. Larsen at home?" I asked. I'd gotten their name off the mailbox.

"Where else would he be?" she asked. There was

a trace of an Irish accent, I thought, or perhaps English. It was early afternoon and already her words were somewhat slurred. When I raised my eyebrows questioningly, she motioned me to follow her through the dark, dingy hallway to a room at the back of the house. Mr. Larsen was propped up in a hospital bed, his head lolling to one side, a thin thread of spittle suspended from his chin. His eyes were open but unfocused.

"What happened?" I asked, backing out of the room. The smell of sickness was worse than the dubious aromas in the rest of the house.

She led me back to the living room and offered me a seat. When I saw the stained chair, I was glad I wasn't wearing shorts. She pulled herself up onto the equally dirty sofa, and her legs were so short that her feet stuck straight out in front of her. They looked about three inches long and I tried not to smile.

"I told you he wouldn't be much help," she said, as if it were my fault. "Cancer's got him all over. The doc says it won't be long now. No point in sending him to hospital. Nothing anyone can do. He could go any day now." Her eyes seemed to come alive at the prospect.

"I'm sorry," I said, not knowing what else to say. I got up and went to the curtained window, where what had to be the world's shortest tripod held a rather impressive telescope. I pulled the curtains open and Mrs. Larsen winced.

"Hey! You're hurting my eyes," she complained. "That thing's just for bird watching."

I apologized but kept the curtains open far enough to peer through the telescope. I had to bend over to get my eye on the lens. What I saw surprised me. It was a close-up view of Rick and Towne's bedroom. The bed was center stage. I turned to Mrs. Larsen, who was staring at me defiantly, her arms crossed. I'm afraid my own eyes were wide with disbelief.

"So what!" she finally managed. "It's none of your business what I do in my own home."

"Nor yours what other people do in theirs," I said. I could tell her hands were itching to get hold of that bottle. She kept eyeing the spot where she'd hidden it.

"They should learn to draw their shades, then," she said. She sounded about ten years old. If it weren't for the gray hair and wrinkles, her size and tone might fool someone. I turned the scope slightly, and with a few minor adjustments I was able to zoom in on Hazel Krause's place too. I swung the telescope to the right, and then left, and realized that Mrs. Larsen had the ability to see right into every single house on the ridge. When I turned back, she had finally taken hold of the bottle, and was pouring a rather hefty dollop into a crusty glass on the coffee table.

"Do you own a computer?" I asked, walking toward her. She spilled her drink, and I realized I was intimidating her. For once, I'd run into someone shorter than I was.

"Good heavens, no," she said. "Couldn't afford one even if I wanted one. Why would I want one?" She swallowed some scotch and seemed to relax.

"To write nasty blackmail notes to the neighbors you spy on?" I asked.

Her watery eyes widened. "Blackmail? Why would I want to blackmail anyone?"

"Why do you have your telescope aimed at your neighbors?"

She seemed to consider this. When she answered, I realized with a pang of guilt that she had started to weep. "What else is there to do?" she wailed. "The TV reception's no good up here, because of the ridge. I can't go anywhere with him in there. I've got no family left. What would you have me do? Kill myself?"

Oh, great. Now it was my fault if she decided to do herself in. She was pathetic, really, and I did feel sorry for her, even if she was a peeping Tom.

"Mrs. Larsen, I don't believe you're blackmailing anyone. But someone is, and it occurs to me that you might be able to help. Have you seen anyone other than the mailman put mail in the boxes across the way?"

She sniffed and wiped her nose on her sleeve. "I might have. I don't rightly recall."

"What might help you recall?" I asked, wondering how much money I had on me. I started to dig in my pocket, but she waved me off.

"Don't insult me," she said. "I don't need bribing. It's just that my memory isn't as sharp as it used to be. Sometimes I remember things all of a sudden, like. Maybe if you came by again tomorrow, I might remember more. I'm not feeling well at all today. And, if you wanted to, you could pick up a bottle of Cutty Sark. Just if you wanted."

She was playing me for a fool, and I doubted she

remembered anything worth following up on, but it might be worth the price of a bottle of booze to find out. I thanked her for her help and told her to start thinking about anything she might have seen that could help me in my investigation. I left feeling grateful for the cool, clean air outside, taking great, greedy gulps all the way down to my boat.

By the time I got home, it was after noon. Clouds had started to crowd the horizon and I wondered if a new storm was on the way. Gammon and Panic were thrilled to see me, and the three of us spent the rest of the day fooling around in the back yard. Panic caught a giant mole that had been digging dirt mounds in the lawn, while Gammon watched lazily from the porch. It was a restful afternoon, and by dinnertime, I knew what I wanted to do.

When Jess answered the phone, I didn't waste any time with small talk. "Didn't Jessie used to be a Girl Scout?" I asked. He agreed that this was true. "And didn't they hike up that ridge for an overnight campout?" Again, he concurred. "Do you think she might remember the way well enough to show me the path?"

The silence that met this question lasted quite a while. When he spoke, he was all business. "It could be dangerous, Cass."

How could I assure him that I'd never do anything to put Jessie in danger? We both knew that sometimes things got out of control. "It was a stupid idea," I said. "Forget it."

"Now wait a minute, Cass. I didn't say no. I was just thinking out loud. You know she's been dying to help you out. This might be just the thing."

"I only need her to show me the path up. Once

we get there, I'll leave her in a nice safe place until I've had a chance to look around. But it would mean she'd miss a day of school."

He laughed. "I'm sure that would break her heart. Let me put her on. You'll have to ask her."

Which meant it was a done deal.

I told Jessie my plan and she leaped at it.

"I'm not sure I remember the exact way," she said excitedly. "It was two years ago. But I'm sure between the two of us, we can find the path."

I told her I'd pick her up at the county dock at eight the next morning and I could feel her huge grin all the way across the telephone line. Getting to miss a day of school was an added bonus.

I fixed myself a grilled chicken breast in a lime and tomatillo sauce, with a broiled tomato and some white rice. It was a good meal, which I enjoyed with a glass of dry Pinot Noir. I don't buy the white-wine-with-chicken idea. It is my firm belief that a good Pinot or Cab goes with almost anything, cold cereal being the possible exception. The truth was, despite making a big show of enjoying my meal, I was feeling rather lonely. And so, after dinner, against my better judgment, I dialed Erica's number.

The phone rang four times before it was answered by a deep, sexy voice. It wasn't Erica.

"Uh, yes, is Erica Trinidad there?" I asked, my heart sinking.

"She's in the other room. Can I take a message?"

The other room, meaning the shower, I supposed. And I'd bet a million dollars that the owner of the bedroom voice was Erica's famous movie director.

"No, no message," I said, banging the receiver down a little louder than I'd intended.

I spent the rest of the evening punishing myself with exercise. I rode the stationary bike for an hour and then went through all of the self-defense and martial arts moves I'd ever learned. I stretched and kicked until my limbs ached. I even meditated. And none of it helped one bit.

Chapter Ten

Monday morning, Jessie was waiting for me at the dock, her bright red tennis shoes a beacon for me in the heavy fog. I was glad to see she'd worn a sweat shirt and jeans. It might warm up before we were through, but at the moment, it was downright chilly.

She chattered happily the whole trip over to Cedar Ridge, and it was slow going in the fog, so by the time we got there, I knew more about the inner tickings of the sixth-grade class at Cedar Hills Elementary School than I'd ever cared to. We passed Rick and Towne's place and went around the tip of the peninsula to the other side which had no houses on its sloped, rocky face.

"It's right up there," she said, pointing to a small cove with about ten feet of sandy beach. "That's where they dropped us off." I raised the prop on my Sea Swirl so as not to drag bottom and eased the boat up onto the sand. Jessie hopped out and I tossed her the bow line, which she managed to tie to a willow branch. I had brought a couple of backpacks and as we put them on, I studied the steep climb ahead of us.

"You sure this is where you went up?" I asked, wondering what kind of sadistic mind would make Girl Scouts scale this monstrous rock.

"I think so," she said. "Come on!" It was hard to resist her enthusiasm.

The path was actually pretty good in places and seemed to have been recently traveled. Where dirt covered the granite, boot prints could be seen. These would have been washed away by the recent storm, I thought. So someone had been up here since Thursday. There were other signs, too, of recent habitation. Cigarette butts, a Coke can and even a glob of chewing gum on a flat rock told me quite a few people had been traveling this very path.

"Do the Scouts still use this?" I asked. Jessie didn't know, but it didn't seem likely now that Reverend Love had bought the property.

About halfway up, Jessie and I peeled off our sweatshirts and stuffed them into our backpacks. We shared a bottle of Evian spring water and wiped the sweat from our foreheads. Our T-shirts were already stuck to our backs, and the bright sun had finally penetrated the fog, which didn't help.

"We're almost there," Jessie said, watching me assess the climb remaining. "We went a lot slower with the Scouts," she added.

"Is this too fast?" I asked, hoping. We had been pushing pretty hard.

"No way!" She started off ahead of me. "Come on!" My legs were starting to feel the abuse I'd inflicted on them the night before, but I was damned if I'd let an eleven-year-old get the better of me.

Because the hill was so steep, the path curved around and around, through the towering cedar and Douglas fir, crossing tiny streams and sometimes hugging the perilous edge of the cliff. Looking down, I could see my boat, a tiny dot of blue on a speck of white. It was better if I didn't look down.

"We're almost to the top," Jessie said. "See that? That didn't used to be there." She was pointing to a tall pole up ahead with what looked like some kind of scope on top. As we drew closer, I noticed that the scope moved with us.

"It's a camera," I whispered. "Like they have in the banks and Seven Elevens." Jessie stared at me blankly and I realized that she'd never been in a Seven Eleven. My California background was creeping up again.

"Maybe we better not go any farther," she said, pointing to a No Trespassing sign.

"Okay," I said. "Here's what I want you to do. Stay right here on this rock, and if you see anyone coming, whistle."

"What do you mean?" she asked, looking a little scared. "Where are you going?"

"I just want to look around. See what kind of

religious retreat the good Reverend is building up here. You stay put."

She didn't appear too happy about this, but she didn't argue.

"If anyone asks what you're doing, we just came up for a hike. Got it?"

She nodded.

"Tell them I had to find a spot to pee and that you're just waiting for me, and then we're going back down."

"I got it, Cassidy. Go on!"

I couldn't help smiling at her impatience as I continued up the path. About every ten feet I passed another No Trespassing sign. It would be hard to convince someone I hadn't seen them.

The trees were indeed huge up here, and I tried to calculate how many trees there could be. I marked off what I thought to be roughly the length and width of a football field. Each tree took nearly ten feet of space, and they grew close together in places. I figured there were nearly one hundred and twenty trees per football field, which according to the equivalency chart in the Almanac I'd studied last night, was about five-sixths of an acre. And Susie Popps had said the whole ridge was just over twenty acres. I wish I'd brought a calculator with me. Jess said a person could get seven hundred dollars for one forty-foot tree. At the very least, these trees would be worth fifteen hundred each. I tried to calculate how much one acre would be worth, but kept getting different numbers. All I knew for sure was, if all the acres were as dense as this one, the Reverend was sitting on several million dollars. And that was without the Douglas fir, let alone one or two of those Port Orford cedar. No wonder he was so anxious to get the road access, I thought. But why hadn't he just paid the neighbors for using their road, I wondered again. Unless he had some reason for not wanting any neighbors at all.

If the first camera surprised me, the next one really got my attention. It was stationed on what looked like a cannon, and it was aimed right at me. Someone had certainly put in a lot of heavy surveillance equipment up here. I smiled innocently at the camera and marched on. I wondered how long it would be before whoever was on the other end of those cameras would come find me.

At last I reached what seemed to be the top of the ridge. From here, the view through the trees was awe-inspiring. The lake looked like a tiny smattering of jewels far below. I could see the ocean, whitewater and all, a mile away. On Highway One, the cars crawled like colorful bugs along a black ribbon. But what really caught my attention was right up on the top of the ridge. Hidden among the trees were dozens of what looked like Quonset huts made of army fatigue material. And off to the south, I could hear the shouts of men, and what sounded like the grunts and groans of heavy exercise.

Ignoring the rapid beating of my heart, I edged forward, scanning the area for any sign of life. As I neared the activity, I passed close to one of the huts and peered in through a screened window. Rows and rows of sleeping bags, tightly coiled, filled the floor of the room. I peered into another hut and saw a similar configuration, except instead of sleeping bags, there were rows of Army surplus duffel bags. I was debating whether or not to risk entering the hut to unzip one of the bags when a twig snapped behind me and I jumped. I whirled around and looked straight into the black eyes of Reverend Love.

"You seem to make a habit of trespassing," he said, his deep voice rolling like thunder.

I tried to keep my own voice from trembling. "Reverend Love! What a surprise!"

I stepped forward to shake his hand. This caught him off guard, and grudgingly he obliged by extending his hand. It was large and cold, like grabbing a lizard barehanded. I resisted the urge to cringe.

"I didn't know there were any buildings up here," I went on. "I used to hike up here all the time. It's one of my favorite places. When I saw the signs, I admit I got curious. I thought this was government-owned land." I was talking a mile a minute, like some bubble-headed moron, but it seemed to be working.

"This land belongs to me now," he said.

"Really?" I said, marveling at how I could make myself sound so innocent and cheerful. "Isn't that exciting. What a lovely spot. Are you planning on building?"

"This is a religious retreat," he said. "Right now, we have a number of devoted followers going through their exercises. It is a private gathering, however. They have been assured there will be no visitors, no interruptions, no intrusions. It is paramount to their success in achieving the inner peace needed to find Divine Love. I'm afraid I'm going to have to ask you to go the way you came. Perhaps we can chat more next Sunday, in church?"

"Well, I've never been a big church-goer myself," I said. I was starting to sweat under my arms. I didn't know whether he was buying my Miss Innocent routine or not, and I was anxious to get out of there. "But you do preach an interesting sermon."

"I'm glad you enjoyed it," he said. "I'm afraid my message may have been lost on many. I understand you're a private investigator."

Man, did that come out of nowhere. And just when I thought he was buying my act. I realized that with my back to the hut, and with him standing in my path, I had no way of escaping if I needed to.

"Well, it's a living," I said, lamely.

"A dangerous one, I understand. Snooping into other people's business can be, er, quite hazardous."

"That's why I carry a gun," I said, wishing I'd brought mine with me. I tapped my waist band, as if that's where my gun was stashed, and smiled sweetly.

"Lots of people have guns," he said, sliding his hand into his own pocket. "Well, have a nice day."

"You too, Reverend," I said, slipping past him. I could almost feel his eyes burning the back of my head as I walked away, even after I knew I was out of sight. It took every ounce of courage I could muster to stop myself from running.

Jessie was right where I'd left her, crouched on her rock, her eyes wide with worry behind her wire-framed glasses.

"What took you so long?" she demanded.

104

"Come on, let's get out of here. I'll tell you later."

The whole way down the mountain, I kept picturing those rows of duffel bags, and it occurred to me that they were each about the exact shape and size of a rifle.

Chapter Eleven

After dropping Jessie back at the county dock, I hurried home, in serious need of a shower. My answering machine light was blinking and I listened as I undressed.

"Hey, babe, it's Martha. I checked up on Loveland for you like I promised, and guess what? It would take a degree in corporate law to figure this one out. Loveland seems to be a subsidiary of something called Meyerson Corporation, which is a subsidiary of something called Port Land Company, which is a subsidiary of something else called, get this, the

Christian Commitment. Scary, huh? I did some checking — for which you owe me, by the way, something really fattening — and it looks like the Christian Commitment has ties to another really lovely group, this one a little more well known. Any guesses? Try the K.K.K. Neat guy, your Reverend." She paused. "Anyway, that's about as far as I got, but at least we've got a better idea of who you're dealing with. I'm talking chocolate mousse, at the very least, Cassidy, or maybe even something flambéd. See you, babe." The message ended a second before the long beep sounded to indicate her time was up. Martha had an uncanny knack of knowing just how long her messages could be.

The second call was from Sheriff Booker, and he sounded excited.

"Cass, it looks like our friend the Reverend just doesn't exist. There's no Reverend Love, or even Robert Love which is what his lease on the church says his name is, anywhere on record. Kinda hard to check his arrest records when he doesn't exist. Now, that little Herman Hugh Pittman is another story." Booker coughed, then continued. "It seems he almost did some time about ten years ago for, you're going to love this, detonating a home-made bomb in his neighbor's mailbox. The guy was going to press charges, and because messing with a mailbox is a federal crime, he would have ended up doing some time. But for some reason the whole case got dropped. The only reason I know about it is I talked to the sheriff in Coleman County where Pittman grew up. He says Pittman was always in some kind of trouble, but nothing ever stuck. Said the last he heard, Pittman had teamed up with some right-wing group in Idaho. I checked with Ed Beechcomb over at the post office, and he said Herman's a real good worker. I'm gonna go have a chat with the little turd and see if he can shed some light on the Reverend's real identity. I don't like not knowing who's preaching in my town, and —"

The sheriff, who talked slower than Martha, was cut off by the long beep and I had to chuckle as I headed for the shower.

I thought about the news they'd delivered. It wasn't cheering. What I had was a creep who could make bombs, with the temperament to blow up his neighbor's mailbox, and who seemed to be teamed up with some phony posing as a reverend who had ties to the K.K.K. Not only had the Reverend just bought twenty acres of timberland worth several million dollars, but it seemed likely he was blackmailing people in order to get their road access. And to top it off, he also seemed to be housing large groups of men on the top of a mountain, for purposes I couldn't fathom. Perfectly legal, yet somehow I didn't think they were there for any religious retreat.

If I was right about him not wanting any neighbors, then it followed that he was up to something illegal. But what? And where did the people I heard up there come from? I could imagine a few locals spending their weekends at a religious retreat, or even a male-consciousness gathering, but this was Monday. Why weren't those people working? And who were they? If even half of them had been from Cedar Hills, people in town would be talking. Was the Reverend some kind of Robert Bly wannabe? At this point, I had more questions than answers.

By the time I'd dressed and blow-dried my hair, I

was ravenous. I was also convinced that I needed to get another look at the top of the ridge, but with all that surveillance equipment, I'd have to find another route.

I poked around in the fridge and started laying things on the counter. I decided a sandwich sounded good, so I hollowed out a sourdough roll the size of a small sub and slathered mayonnaise over the insides. To this I spooned generous amounts of olive oil, chopped green olives, sliced tomatoes which I salted and peppered, diced red bell pepper, a handful of dill pickle slices and a tiny bit of chopped red onion. I laid on about five slices of salami, some provolone and, for good measure, a little Tillamook cheddar. I opened a bottle of Red Dog beer, grabbed a handful of napkins and invited the cats to join me out on the front deck. After careful consideration, the three of us came to the unanimous decision that this was indeed one of the top ten sandwiches we'd ever shared.

Chapter Twelve

After my lunch, I napped, then puttered about in the yard. The creek that runs under my house had overrun its banks during the recent storm, and I used a hoe to smooth out the banks, replacing the rocks that bordered the creek. By the time I finished, I had to go meet Jessie's shrink. I changed into tan slacks, a plaid cotton vest over a white button-up blouse, and a pair of soft leather loafers. For some reason, I felt I needed to dress for the occasion. I ran a brush through my hair, noting that it could use a trim, and smiled at my reflection. Not bad, I thought, wondering why I was getting spruced up for a psychologist.

Dr. Carradine's place was really just an old brick house that had been converted into an office building. A red brick chimney jutted out of the second-floor roof, and the windows were framed with window boxes crammed with red geraniums and white petunias. There was an "open" sign on the white front door, so I pushed it open and tentatively entered a cozy waiting room. It was empty.

"Be right with you!" a voice called from around the corner. There were chairs artfully arranged around end tables laden with dozens of magazines, ash trays and even a couple of candy dishes filled with mints. I popped a mint into my mouth, checking first to make sure no one was looking. The walls were decorated with good paintings, and I recognized one as Rick's — a giant red hibiscus flower with yellow pollen buds in the center. An iridescent green hummingbird, dwarfed by the giant flower, drank to its heart's content. I was still staring at the painting when I heard someone behind me. I turned around, and my heart dropped down to my shoes.

"Oh, God," she said.

"You!" I managed. My mouth had gone suddenly dry.

"Isn't this a surprise?" she said, making the understatement of the century. Her green eyes, as deep and lovely as I remembered, twinkled with humor. And something else, too. I wondered if I looked as dumbstruck as I felt.

"I had no idea," I said. "Obviously."

"Nor I," she said. "I wondered if I'd ever see you again. I have to admit, I've thought about you quite a bit."

Her straightforwardness was a bit unsettling.

"I, uh, have thought of you too," I said truthfully. "I've kicked myself a dozen times for not at least getting your name."

"Maggie Carradine," she said, walking over to me, extending her hand. Her gaze was riveting, and I couldn't take my eyes off her. Her hand was warm, her grip strong and gentle at the same time.

"Cassidy James," I said, and we both laughed at the absurdity of the situation.

"Come on in, Cassidy James," she said, finally letting go of my hand. I followed her lovely backside into her office which must have at one time been a living room. One large window looked out onto the harbor. The walls were painted a muted rose, and on them hung a number of wonderful paintings, all of them Rick's.

"He told me you were a loyal customer," I said, gazing at the huge canvases.

"You know Rick Parker?" she asked.

"Actually, we just met."

"What a small world!" she exclaimed.

"And my best friend is Martha Harper," I added, enjoying her look of surprise.

"And of course, you know Jess and Jessie, too," she said, shaking her head. "Even in Kings Harbor, that's a lot of coincidence. How is it we haven't met?"

"We have," I reminded her. The blush that crept

up her face and spread down her chest matched the way my own face felt. We stood gazing at each other, neither of us sure what to do next.

"You're not at all what I expected," she said, finally, sitting down in a soft leather chair. I sat too, suddenly glad I'd dressed up for this particular shrink.

"I mean, aside from your turning out to be the woman I've been thinking about for the past forty-eight hours, you're not what I thought a private investigator would be like."

"And what was that?" I asked, genuinely curious. She pushed the black curls off her forehead and tapped a pencil against her teeth, thinking. She was even more attractive than I remembered, I thought, intensely aware of the curves beneath her blazer. She was athletic but also womanly, and I had to fight the urge to let my gaze wander.

"I guess I thought you'd be more butch," she said finally.

"You don't think I'm butch?" I thought of the many times I'd been mistaken for a young boy. I was muscular and lean, with short sandy hair, and when I dressed in jeans and a sweatshirt, I could pass for a sixteen-year-old jock.

"No," she said. "I expected someone harder. More cynical. A pack of Tareytons rolled up in your shirt-sleeve, that kind of thing. Don't ask me why. I guess I'm guilty of stereotyping. I just never figured a P.I. to be so good-looking."

The compliment caught me off guard. "Thank you."

Her laughter was pure and genuine. "Well, I think it's safe to say this is about the most unprofessional conversation I've ever had in this room."

"Well, it's not like I came here as a client," I said, feeling suddenly self-conscious.

"That's true," she said. "And I really do want to talk about Jessie. Why don't we do that, and then we can discuss other things afterwards."

She started by telling me what she knew, and I filled in details as she went. How had Jessie reacted after she'd shot her brother, she wanted to know. I told her she had fainted. Did she talk about her brother, she asked. I told her she referred to the incident, but never mentioned Dougie's name. Did I think Jessie was coping well, adjusting? I said I thought Jessie was the most well adjusted eleven-year-old I knew. I thought she was handling it better than her father was, or even better than I was.

"You're not handling it well?" she asked. It was a typical shrink question, and red flags went up all over the place.

"I'm doing okay," I said.

"But you have guilt about what happened," she said. It wasn't phrased as a question. I started to get defensive, then thought better of it.

"I guess that's part of it," I said. "It was my first case. I had found out about the fort from Jessie. That's probably why she followed her dad, who was following me out there. She knew where I was going. So in a way, I was responsible for her being there. Then, as you pointed out earlier, I'm supposed to be the rough, tough P.I. Only instead, I end up having to toss my gun, strip naked and am about to get raped by some giant idiot on steroids, when little Jessie steps in to save the day. I'd have been dead if she hadn't been there. So would her father." Despite my best efforts to remain calm, the recounting of the incident brought up emotions I'd refused to dwell on, and I feared any minute my eyes would well up with tears. This was exactly why I didn't like shrinks, I reminded myself.

"I think it's very natural to feel guilt, even when in our heads we know there was nothing we could have done differently. You didn't choose to throw your gun away. From what I understand, they had a knife on your friend." For some reason, I'd intentionally left Erica out of the story. "And," she went on, "you didn't invite the boys to rape you. In that situation, anyone would have been helpless."

"But I'm not supposed to be helpless!" I said more adamantly than I'd intended. "I shouldn't have gotten myself and everyone else into that situation," I added calmly.

"I didn't realize," she said, "that when they gave you the private investigator's license, they also awarded you omnipotence." Her smile was wry but her eyes were kind, and I couldn't decide if I was mad at her or not. She saved me from answering by changing the subject. "Jessie seems to idolize you. A little of that can be healthy. Sometimes it isn't."

"You think it isn't with me?" I asked, my heart sinking. I loved that kid.

"I'm not sure. She has this romanticized vision of you as the slayer of evil. You know she wants to be a cop. I'm afraid, after 'saving the day' as you put it, she thinks that now she is also omnipotent. It doesn't help that she thinks that is a realistic goal."

"Meaning what?" I asked, starting to squirm.

"Meaning I think it might be a good idea for you to let her see you in a realistic light. Let her see the flaws, the weaknesses, the vulnerability. She needs to know that it's okay to cry. It's okay to be scared. It's okay to fail. Right now, she is setting herself up for a hard fall. A lot of really smart kids put undue pressure on themselves to succeed. Not only is Jessie unusually bright, but the incident with her brother has caused her to see herself as invulnerable to pain, immune to failure. High achievers make up one of the highest percentages of teen suicides. I just don't want Jessie to become one of them."

Jesus! Talk about guilt. All of the sudden, I was responsible for Jessie's life. How did that happen, I wondered. I didn't want that responsibility. Maggie must have read my thoughts.

"I'm not saying she's your responsibility. I just thought you should be aware of the importance you hold in her life. It would be to her benefit if you were a little less God-like and a little more human. So she could let herself be human too."

It made sense and I knew it. I wondered how Maggie could know so much about me, just from listening to Jess and Jessie. Did Jess see me that way too? God-like? Sure, I put on a big show of being in control and confident. But I didn't think I came across as all-knowing. Did I? Was that the way people saw me? Gee, I must be a ton of fun to be around.

I got up and circled the room, looking from one painting to another, my mind reeling. Martha had been right, Rick's paintings did inspire introspection. But I was in no mood to bare my soul to a shrink.

Even this shrink. Even looking in those sea-green eyes that filled me with a strange mixture of serenity and longing. I would work this thing out on my own, in my own good time.

"I went too far, didn't I?" Maggie said. She had come up behind me and was standing looking over my shoulder at a large picture of a field of pansies. A spotted fawn stood at the far edge of the field, nearly hidden in the oversized flowers, nibbling away. I could smell Maggie's perfume, almost feel her breath on my shoulder. "I do that sometimes," she said. "I wasn't thinking about your feelings. I got carried away. I'm sorry." This didn't sound like a shrink talking. It sounded like a friend.

"But you were right," I said, surprising myself.

I turned to face her, and was further surprised to feel the tears in my eyes. I hated crying. I had no idea why I should be crying, but her smile was so sweet, I didn't try to hide them.

"The person you described, that you don't want Jessie to have to try to be, that's me. Straight A's in school. Best student athlete. Lettered in every sport. Youngest person to get a master's degree in my class. Teacher of the Year my second year teaching. Blah, blah, blah. My first lover accused me of being Little Ms. Perfect. It infuriated me at the time, but I knew she was right. After she died, I dropped out. I quit everything. Moved out here to live in peace. I was tired of succeeding at everything I did. And then Martha talked me into becoming a P.I., and it seemed like the perfect fit. No expectations, no rules, no pressure. Except, of course, that the pressure has always been self-inflicted. And still is. I can't just be a private investigator, Maggie. I have to be the best one that ever lived. I don't just cook dinner. I do gourmet. It's a character flaw, I admit, but I never thought it was hurting anyone else. Now you tell me that I'm probably screwing up the only kid I really like, and I'm at a loss for what to do. How do I change now?" The tears had actually started to slide down my cheek, and Maggie reached out and wiped them away with her hand. I was pretty sure this wasn't standard psychotherapy procedure.

"You don't need to change who you are, Cassidy. Just let people see your vulnerabilities. You do have some, I'm sure." She smiled, and so did I. She was making fun of me, but she did it so kindly it didn't hurt.

"Maybe one or two," I admitted, wiping the rest of the tears away. "I don't usually cry like this, you know."

"I know," she said. "It's not a bad start. So, just how gourmet do you get, anyway?" she asked, lightening things up.

"Well, I don't do veal," I said, "on account of it being so politically incorrect, although just between you and me, I adore it. And I have trouble with bunnies and lambs. But other than that, I pretty much cook everything. I have my old favorites, but what I really love is to try new recipes. I love French food, Mexican food, Italian food, you name it. The only thing I like better than cooking a great meal is having someone else cook one for me. I'm an equal opportunity glutton."

"Can you handle non-gourmet stuffed bell peppers?" she asked. "I've got some already in the oven. I live upstairs. I'd love for you to stay for dinner."

I told her I'd be delighted, and I was. We climbed the stairs, me appreciating the way she moved the whole way up, marveling at how much better I felt. Perhaps I should cry more often, I thought. She unlocked the front door and led me into an airy, inviting room. The view of the harbor was wonderful, and the furniture seemed comfortable and well lived in. The hardwood floor was dotted with colorful throw rugs, and there was artwork everywhere. Maggie flipped on the stereo, and the room was filled with the rich, mellow tones of Nina Simone.

"I'll be just a minute," she said. "Make yourself at home."

I reminded myself I was not here on a case, but it was hard to resist my natural tendency to snoop. There were dozens of sculptures, some of cats but most of nude women. Maggie, I decided, had excellent taste. On one wall there was nothing but black and white photographs. Most of them were action shots — one or two of a woman on a sailboard, a half dozen of a woman rapelling down a mountainside, suspended in midair by one thin rope, and one of a goggled woman racing downhill on skis. I realized with a start that all of them were of Maggie.

"I hope you like Cabernet," she said, coming up behind me and resting her hand on my shoulder. The touch sent a jolt right through me.

I took the glass and smiled. "I love Cabernet," I said. "How good are you?"

"I beg your pardon?" she stammered, blushing.

"At rock climbing." I pointed my chin at the photographs.

"Oh, that," she said. "Thank God. I thought you were getting fresh."

"Later," I said. We both laughed.

"It's one of my passions. I'm actually pretty accomplished. Last year I scaled Mount Picacho. Why do you ask?"

"Can you teach me?" I asked excitedly. Before she could answer, I added, "tomorrow night? After dark?"

"What?" She didn't seem to know whether or not to take me seriously.

"I need to find a way up a very small mountain," I said. "It's really just a big rock. But it's straight up, unless you go along the path. And I've already done that." I told her about taking Jessie up to the top of the ridge, and about the surveillance equipment, the tents and the Reverend. I had never broken a client's confidentiality and I didn't intend to now, but because I thought it might help convince her, I told her about two gay men being blackmailed by someone I was convinced was the bogus Reverend. I didn't leave anything about him out. When I finished, she went to get us more wine.

"So you want me to take you up the side of this rock, as you put it, in total darkness, even though you've never done any mountain climbing in your life?"

"I'm a fast learner," I said. "And I'm in good shape."

"I can see that," she said wryly, eyeing me up and down. I felt my face grow hot but held my composure. I needed her to agree.

"And," she continued, "you want me to do this even though you suspect that the people at the top of this ridge, which we'll be invading in the middle of the night, are armed and dangerous. Does that about cover it?"

"I wouldn't expect you to come all the way up," I said, sheepishly. "Just get me close enough to the top so that I can get up there, and then wait for me to come back. I just want to look around without those cameras seeing me. I won't be up there for more than just a few minutes."

She laughed heartily, her green eyes flashing with humor. "What a charmer!" she said. "How can I resist? Tell me, do you always get your way so easily with women?"

"Usually," I said, grinning, getting up to face her. I took her wine glass and set it on the table, next to my own. Her face was warm and smooth. I let my fingers explore the satiny skin of her cheeks and neck before I drew her closer and touched her lips with my own. They parted, soft and wonderful, letting me kiss her passionately, kissing me back. The timer buzzed from the kitchen and she pulled away reluctantly, trailing her fingertips down between my breasts to my stomach before pulling away. If she'd had any idea what that did to me, she wouldn't have left me that way. Like a faithful puppy, I followed her into the kitchen.

"Let me just take these out of the oven," she said, reaching up with a pot holder. Before she could finish, I reached around her, turned the oven off and closed the oven door.

"Later," I said, turning her to face me, embarrassed at the huskiness of my voice. I pressed up against her, sensing the sudden response of her nipples under her blouse. My lips found hers again, and this time the kiss was so ardent that I feared I was hurting her back by pressing her against the kitchen counter. But the sounds she made told me that what she felt was not pain.

I was not gentle, but I couldn't help it. Hungrily, I slid my hands over her body, reveling in the soft warmth of her breasts, the heat of her body. I felt, rather than heard, each moan, the sharp intake of breath, the growing excitement. My own excitement was unbearable, and I came with shuddering gasps when I felt her exquisite release.

It had happened too fast. It had been too rough. I was embarrassed at the urgency I'd felt. I was mortified. We were still dressed and standing in the damned kitchen, for God's sake. So how come I felt so ridiculously happy, I wondered, marveling at my own conflicting emotions.

"What's so funny?" Maggie asked, holding me at arm's length so that she could see my face.

"I'm embarrassed," I said.

"As well you should be," she teased. "What was that? A world record? You could write a book. *The Ten-Second Orgasm.*" I was beginning to like her humor. It would take a strong woman to put up with it though. It tended to be directed at me. Then again, I thought of myself as a pretty strong woman.

"It was just a prelude," I said, regaining a little of my usual cockiness. "I didn't want your dinner to go cold."

"What dinner?" Maggie asked, a sultry smile on her lips. "Come on."

She took my hand and led me to her bedroom, where neither of us thought about the dinner again for a good portion of the night. By the time we did, we were too exhausted to care.

Chapter Thirteen

The sleep, what little there was of it, was sound. I was lying face down, sprawled in tangled sheets, still half asleep, when the aroma of freshly ground coffee invaded my senses. I squinted against the light and saw Maggie's smiling face leaning over me. So it hadn't been a dream, I thought, grinning. I'd been afraid it had been too good to be true.

"I've got a client waiting downstairs," she said, brushing her lips against my forehead. "Stay as long as you want. I'll call you later."

She started to turn, but I reached out and pulled

her back down until she was nearly lying on top of me. She was wearing a tan silk blouse tucked into a matching skirt, and when I ran my hands across the silky fabric, I could feel her immediate response.

"Cass," she whispered, burying her nose in my neck. "We can't."

She was as soft and warm as I remembered, and I couldn't stop myself from sliding my hand beneath the short skirt, feeling the silky texture of her thighs, the even silkier texture of her panties.

"Cass," she whispered again, her voice husky with desire. "I have a client downstairs." Her words were separated by shallow intakes of breath as I let my hand slide higher, feeling her quickening response to each movement. "We really can't," she breathed, beginning to move against my hand. But we could, and we did. The shuddering gasps rocked us both, and we lay together breathing heavily into each other's hair, hearts pounding in unison.

"That's for that little comment you made about the ten-second orgasm," I said when I'd finally caught my breath.

She responded by biting my neck, not an unpleasant sensation.

"I'll never be able to keep a straight face downstairs." She pushed herself from the bed and straightened her clothes. I propped myself up and watched her, grinning like a fool. She was lovely with or without clothes. "I don't dare kiss you good-bye," she said, standing with her hands on her hips in mock anger.

"I promise," I said, holding my hands up innocently. "I won't even touch you once." She leaned over and planted a chaste kiss on my lips. "I lied," I said, putting my arms around her. I pulled her back down, kissing her deeply. When we both started to respond, I let go, but she didn't move away.

"I'm going to miss you today," she murmured.

"I already miss you," I answered. And it was true. Watching her walk out the door left me feeling both sad and ridiculously happy.

I retrieved my clothes which somehow had strewn themselves around the room, and I made the bed. I could smell her perfume on the pillows and found it terribly arousing. I took a few sips of the coffee she'd brought me, and with one last glance at the bed, I let myself out into an overcast day and found myself whistling all the way to my Jeep.

When I got home both cats were stomping mad. "Where have you been?" they meowed. "Whose scent is that all over you?" they demanded. "Where is our breakfast?" Gammon cried.

That, at least, I could do something about. After popping open a can of Kitty Gourmet and spooning it into their dish, I checked my messages. I was taken aback by the voice that came over the line.

"Cassidy? Hi, it's Erica. Where have you been? Listen, I need to talk to you. I know I haven't been very communicative lately. In fact, I've been awful. I want to make it up to you, though. And I have a lot to tell you, too. Call me, okay? I miss you." I stood staring at the phone after the long beep sounded.

"Erica Trinidad," I said aloud, "you have really lousy timing."

I showered and fixed myself a piece of toast, somehow having lost my appetite. My mind was in turmoil and my insides churned. Images of Maggie and me just hours earlier filled my senses, and yet Erica's voice had sent me straight back to earlier images of similar passion. I couldn't return her call. Not yet. I needed to figure out what the hell I was doing. When the phone rang again, I almost didn't answer it. What if it was Erica calling back? What would I say to her? Finally, on the fifth ring, I snatched up the phone.

"Ms. James?"

"Speaking."

"This is Hazel Krause. You must do something! This time, they've gone too far!" Her voice was wavery, on the verge of hysteria.

"What happened?" I asked. "Where are you?" She sounded like she was at a football game.

"I'm at the marina," she wailed. "They tried to kill me, I'm sure of it! And poor little Tommy took the brunt of it." She sounded as if she were about to sob.

"Mrs. Krause, I'll be right over. But please, tell me what happened."

"I came into town to get some groceries," she said, sniffing. "I was only gone about an hour. When I got back, I asked Tommy to fill up the boat with gas, which he did, and then he started the engine for me. Normally, I would have done that myself. But I'd forgotten the milk in the front seat of my car and I ran back up to get it. I was only halfway up the ramp when I heard the explosion. I turned around, and there was Tommy, flying through the air like a rocket. My whole boat is demolished."

"What about Tommy?" I said, trying to stifle my own panic.

"He's got terrible burns! The ambulance is here

now. He's alive though. Thank God for that. I know that bomb was meant for me!"

"Bomb?" My heart was racing.

"What else could it have been?" she asked, her voice near breaking.

"I'll be right there, Mrs. Krause. Stay put."

I flew down the walkway to my boat and tore across the water toward the marina. Boats did blow up, I told myself. There were warnings written right in the cockpit telling you to use the blower for a full five minutes before starting the engine, because you never knew when gas fumes would build up and the tiniest spark could blow the whole boat sky high. It had happened before. Most people, myself included, tended to get lazy. When I did use the blower, it was seldom for the full five minutes. Often, I bypassed this safety measure entirely. Like now, I thought, making a silent promise to start using the blower in the future.

But in the back of my mind, I kept thinking about what the sheriff had said about Herman Hugh's past experience with homemade bombs, and I couldn't help wondering if he hadn't tried to hurry Hazel Krause into leaving the ridge, permanently.

The debris from the boat was all the way out in the channel leading to the marina. I made my way past bits of aluminum, pieces of Fiberglas and swatches of canvas. The dock was crowded with people, and there was no way I was going to get my boat anywhere near the dock itself. I maneuvered my way through the mess, and ended up tying onto someone else's boat in the very last slip. Climbing over the bow, I leaped onto the other boat, and then jumped ashore. I made my way through the noisy

128

crowd and headed straight for Booker, who seemed to be shouting orders at everyone.

"How's Tommy?" I asked, ignoring the looks from those I'd elbowed past.

"Lucky," Booker answered, his usually handsome face frowning. "The kid's got burns on both his legs and upper torso, but his face is fine. If he'd been sitting in the front seat instead of reaching in through the open window to turn that key, he'd be out there with all that floating junk, in little pieces. As it is, he's gonna be fine."

"Thank God," I said, incredibly relieved. "Have you seen Mrs. Krause?"

"She the owner?" he asked. I nodded, faced with a tough decision. Booker knew that I had tied the Reverend and probably Herman Hugh to the blackmail scheme. And he knew Herman Hugh made bombs. What he didn't know was that Hazel Krause was one of the blackmail victims. And my client. To whom I owed and had promised confidentiality. I'd nearly breached that confidence by telling Maggie about the case. I couldn't in good conscience do that again. It was a matter of ethics. But if I didn't tell Booker, he'd probably be looking at this as another case of someone not turning on their engine blower. Biting my lower lip, I took a plunge.

"You think this might have been a bomb?" I asked, trying to sound nonchalant.

"A bomb? Where'd you get that idea?"

"Just a thought."

"Cassidy James," he said, his eyes boring into me, "if you know something, you by God better spit it out." Tom Booker was my friend. But he was also the sheriff.

"I can't break a client's confidentiality," I whispered.

He leaned closer, pretending to squint at the boat's remains. "The owner of this boat is your client?"

I nodded, feeling miserable.

"The one being blackmailed to leave the ridge?" he continued, incredulous.

Again, I nodded.

"You think this is part of that?" he asked. I met his eyes and held the gaze. I wasn't saying anything, but the message was clear. "Well, Jesus H. Christ!" he muttered, shoving a toothpick into the side of his mouth. "Hells bells." He looked up at the steely gray sky. When Booker got agitated, his vocabulary was reduced to curses and clichés.

"I've got to go check on my client," I said. "I'd appreciate it if you wouldn't let on you know about the blackmailing."

"Hey, Cassie. Just because I'm a man doesn't mean I'm a completely insensitive S.O.B." He feigned a hurt look and I smiled.

"Thanks, Tom," I said.

"Thank you, Cass. As soon as I can get a bomb squad over here from Kings Harbor to check this out, I'm gonna want to chat with your client. Keep her around, will you?"

"Sure thing." I turned to push my way through the milling crowd in search of Hazel Krause.

It didn't take me long to realize, however, that Hazel had already left. Her car was gone and so was she. I couldn't blame her, really. The thought that someone had likely tried to kill her would be enough to send anyone running, including me. One way or the other, I thought, the Reverend was getting what he wanted. The only people left on the ridge now were Rick and Towne. I doubted Hazel Krause was coming back any time soon.

Chapter Fourteen

I considered telling Booker about my plans to scale the ridge that night, but I knew he'd try to talk me out of it, and it was something I thought needed to be done. I thought about calling Martha, but I wasn't ready to talk to her about Maggie, and Martha had a way of knowing when I was keeping something from her. It would only be a matter of minutes before she'd have the whole story, and then I'd have to endure all sorts of razzing and probing questions about just how good it was. And then of course she'd ask the twenty-four-thousand-dollar question about Erica, and that was something I just wasn't ready to face.

So instead of calling either Booker or Martha, I called Maggie and we spent a little time going over the plans for that evening, and quite a lot of time murmuring nice things to each other about the night before. Then I called Rick and told him what Maggie and I were going to do.

"I didn't mention your names," I assured him.

"Why on earth not? For heavens sake, Cassidy. Call her right back and tell her everything. And then the two of you can have dinner here before you make the climb. Oh, wait until I tell Towne!"

It wasn't a bad idea. We could walk up their road past the rest of the houses toward the base of the ridge and start the climb from there. I thanked Rick and told him we'd see them at seven.

I found the number for Hazel Krause's son in Kings Harbor and got his wife. After considerable trouble convincing her that I was indeed a friend, she told me that yes, Mrs. Krause had come to stay with them for a while, and that she would not be returning to the lake this summer. I left my name and number, careful not to reveal my identity as a P.I., and asked her to have Hazel call me when she felt up to it. The least I could do was return her money, I thought, feeling lousy and responsible for what may well have been a murder attempt on my client.

I knew that Maggie would say this was another example of my thinking I was omnipotent, but damn it, I did feel responsible. While I was off screwing my brains out, my client's blackmailers were out running around plotting murder. Not that I could prove it yet. But maybe after tonight things would be different, I thought, deciding that this was a good time to get in some target practice.

I made sure the cats were safely indoors and took my .38 out back. I followed the creek up the steep ravine to a clearing where'd I'd set up bales of hay for a firing range. Martha had helped me clear the area and drag up the bales, and every now and then the two of us would climb up there to get in some target practice. We usually made a competition of it, with the stakes being anything from a fancy dessert if I lost — Martha couldn't cook worth beans — to a back rub, Martha's specialty. Martha had begun as a much better shot than I, but I'd been gaining on her, and she accused me of practicing behind her back, which I did, of course, every chance I got. As much as I had fought the idea of getting a gun at first, I found that I actually liked the act of aiming and hitting a target.

The one time I'd really needed a gun on a case, I'd been forced to lay it down, and I knew that being the best shot in the world wouldn't help one bit if I didn't have the guts to use it in the right situation. The truth was, if and when the time ever came, I wasn't sure I'd be able to pull the trigger. But I felt better just knowing the gun was there, and as I took my stance, pulling off round after round, I knew I'd be taking the gun with me tonight.

I was only half-way through my usual routine when a thought struck me. I raced back into the house and replayed Martha's message, jotting down the names of the corporations affiliated with Loveland. Booker had said that Reverend Love didn't exist in any records. I wondered if, by backtracking through those other corporations, I could find out who he really was.

Since the Meyerson Corporation was the one most closely connected with Loveland, I started there. I knew I could hop in my boat, motor over to the marina, jump in my jeep and drive all the way to the Kings Harbor Library where I might be able to find a list of corporations and their locations, but if I did, I'd never make it back in time to pick up Maggie. And I wanted to know more about the Reverend before we made our climb. One of these days I was going to have to upgrade technologically, I chided myself, not for the first time. My Mac didn't have enough memory to even use the internet efficiently. Like it or not, I was going to have to bite the bullet and buy myself some more advanced equipment.

I called Martha, hoping she'd have the information I needed to get started, but she was gone. So I resorted to good old-fashioned detective skills.

Booker had said that Herman Hugh had been part of a right-wing group in Idaho. It was as good a place to start as any. I found a map of Idaho and began calling the information operator in each of the big cities. By the time I'd worked my way down to small towns, I realized my phone bill was going to be astronomical. But at least the operators were friendly. I finally hit pay dirt in McCall.

"Meyerson Corporation," the young voice trilled. She was chewing gum into the receiver.

"Yes, hello. I wonder if you could help me? I'm calling from the All Saints Memorial Hospital in Eugene, Oregon and we have a patient who's just been admitted with a head trauma."

"Uh huh?"

"We're trying to locate the next of kin, but are unable to do so on account of the patient is unconscious and his identification is missing. It appears the poor man has been robbed and beaten."

"Uh huh?" She'd quit smacking her gum, so I knew she was listening.

"The only thing we've been able to recover is this phone number, so I'm hoping perhaps someone there can help us identify the victim. Shall I describe him for you?"

"Who'd you say you were?"

I repeated the hospital bit, throwing in the title of Doctor.

"Just a sec."

While I was on hold, I was treated to a monotonous string of golden oldies. I'd even started to hum along when she came back on the line.

"Mr. Barry is out of the office. But his secretary says to take down the description and we'll get back to you if we can help."

"The thing is, see, time is of the essence. I can hold, if you'd just see if anyone there recognizes the description." Before she could argue, I described Reverend Love in detail.

"Oh my God!" she said. "Is he going to make it?"

"Do you know him then?"

"Mary! It's that Reverend Lowell!" she yelled. Then she said to me, "He used to have a church outside of town here. He worked for Mr. Barry during the week."

"First name?" I was writing furiously.

"Gosh, I don't know. Everyone just called him Reverend."

"Do you have his address or phone number? Is there someone we can contact?"

"Just a sec." This time she didn't bother putting me on hold and I could hear her flipping Rolodex pages.

"Oh, here it is. Alex Lowell. He was only here a year. Came from a church in Portland. That's the only number we have. I don't think he even had any family. It seemed like that church took up all his time."

"What religion did he preach?" I asked.

She giggled and smacked her gum. "Lord if any of us could figure it out. It wasn't the kind of church a person would just drop in on. Most of us go to the Trinity Lutheran anyway. But he did have himself quite a little following. They were always having these week-long retreats and he'd have to miss work. If one of us had done that, we'd have been canned, but I guess him being a Reverend and all, the boss cut him some slack. Are you worried about last rites?"

"Well, we hope it doesn't come to that, but it's always best to ask. What did Lowell do at Meyerson, anyway?"

"The Reverend? He was in distributing."

"And just what does Meyerson Corporation distribute?" I asked, hoping I hadn't pushed my luck too far. There was a brief pause.

"Firearms," she said.

I hung up just as I heard her ask me to repeat my name. I checked my watch. Unfortunately, the number in Portland would have to wait. It was time to pick up Maggie.

Chapter Fifteen

Maggie looked great in black. Her olive skin and green eyes seemed made for the black turtleneck she wore, and I had trouble not staring at her across the table. Rick was in his element, serving us from the "good china" and trying not to pout over our refusal of the wine he offered. Maggie and I both agreed, we needed all our senses for what lay ahead. We ate a spinach and feta salad with pine nuts, a hunk of sourdough bread and had a glass of lemon water. I'd told Rick that anything heavier than a salad would be too much, and though I suspected he'd sulked a bit, he'd come through like a champ. He was so pleased at the idea of Maggie and me together that I think he'd have been content to serve Cheerios. He kept beaming at us, his eyes all lit up like a kid at Christmas, and even Towne seemed pleased.

"Tell it again," Rick said. "Neither of you had the slightest idea who the other one was when you made the appointment?" He'd heard it three times already.

"Rick, leave them alone," Towne teased. "My God, can't you see you're embarrassing them?"

"I am not," Rick said indignantly. "Am I? Oh, God, I am, aren't I?"

Maggie and I both laughed, and I managed to nudge her foot under the table. I realized that I'd been toeing the leg of the table for ten minutes, thinking it was her. Now that I'd actually managed to reach her foot, I could tell the difference, and it sent my stomach into a sudden succession of somersaults.

"Have you thought about what you'll do, Cass, if they catch you snooping around up there?" Towne asked in his sensible way.

In truth, I'd been avoiding thinking about that.

"They won't catch me," I said. "I plan to be very quiet and very quick. I just want to get a look at what's really going on up there without them knowing it. We should be back down before you even miss us."

"How long will it take to climb up?" Towne asked.

Maggie and I had studied the hill from the boat on the way over and she'd visualized the best route up.

"I'd say no more than half an hour to an hour,

depending on how much we need to rest," she said. What she meant was, depending on how well I was able to keep up.

"So, if you start up there around ten, you should be up no later than eleven. Right?" Towne asked. "Then, if Cass is true to her word and only looks around for ten minutes or so, and it takes you just as long to come back down, you should be here by, let's say just after midnight. Does that sound about right?"

"You have to forgive him," Rick said. "He's been an accountant so long he's forgotten that not everyone is as precise as he is. Sometimes I think he times me in the bathroom."

We all laughed, and Maggie got up to help Rick clear the dishes.

"Don't worry, Towne. We'll be okay," I said. "If we're not back by two in the morning, call Sheriff Booker and Martha Harper. Tell them where we went, and they'll know what to do." I jotted down their numbers and slid the paper over to him. His eyes were filled with concern.

"I'm calling at one, Cass. If you're not back by one o'clock, I'm calling." I couldn't decide if he sounded like a little kid or a concerned parent. Either way, though, it was nice to know someone cared.

As we waited for night to fall, Maggie took me out back and went over my instructions again.

"Now, when I yell, 'On belay!' what am I telling you?" she asked, helping me tie the ropes around me. She had already shown me how the carabiner worked, and how to tie the right knots in case something went wrong.

"It means you've got the piton in the crack, and you're ready to help me up to where you are," I said. "But don't yell too loud. We wouldn't want to alert them that we're coming."

"The sound will travel down the rock," she said. "And anyway, from what you said, they should be on the other side of the ridge. Now don't forget, you don't make one move until you hear me call."

"And once I'm climbing up, I yell, 'Climbing!' " I said. "And if I start to fall, I yell 'Falling!' Right?" She'd already told me this three times.

"Don't get cocky on me, Cass. It could happen. This looks like about a Grade Four climb. I've done harder ones, but no beginner starts on Grade Four. Especially in the dark. I shouldn't even be taking you up there. You'll have to be very careful. Now, what's the rule about the rope?"

"I don't touch it," I said, starting to get nervous. "I use my hands and feet to find the cracks. And I never let myself get spread-eagle with all four limbs extended."

"Good," she said. "But mostly you use your legs. That's where your strength is. And you stay on the cliff by using three points, never four. You use the fourth limb to move forward with. If you're ever using all four to hang on with, you'll be stuck. Now when you get up to where I am, what do you do?"

"Kiss you passionately, and see if I can have my way with you?" I asked. Maggie managed a brief smile before giving me a stern look. "Okay, okay," I said, grinning. " 'Off Belay' and then I start recoiling the ropes. Once you start climbing again, I let the rope out until you reach the next resting spot, where you'll sink another piton, and yell 'On belay!' again."

I was feeling like a school kid trying to pass my oral exams. The real test, though, was the one that had me worried.

Maggie must have sensed my growing uneasiness, because she put her arm around me and squeezed my shoulder. Then she started showing me the various ways to grip the cracks and ledges, making me follow her lead.

"On the way down, we'll be rapelling," she said. "The hardest part will be getting started, because you have to step backwards over the cliff. But you get to use the rope and you don't have to worry about finding cracks or ledges. It's really fun when you get the hang of it." She paused to see if I appreciated the pun. I grimaced and she went on. "Unfortunately, you'll have to go first, so I can't even demonstrate for you. Just take little hops, letting the rope out slowly as you descend. You'll be down the cliff before you know it."

She double-checked the ropes, carabiners, pitons and safety anchors, and I made sure I could feel the comforting bulge of my .38 in the shoulder holster beneath my jacket. Ropes weren't the only safety measure we might be needing, I thought, glad for the mild discomfort of the gun. On the other hand, I was beginning to wonder if we'd make it up the rock at all. It was starting to sound more complicated than I'd thought.

It was almost completely dark when we got to the base of the mountain, and for the first time I started to feel really scared. From where we stood, the ridge looked a mile straight up. The moon sat far over to the east, with only a thin sliver of silver shining faintly across the sky.

Maggie whispered last-minute instructions and began her ascent. The rocky face of the cliff seemed to have plenty of footholds, and I tried to watch where she placed her hands and feet as she scrambled up. She made it look easy, but I doubted I could do the same.

Before long, I could hear her far above me, pounding her piton into a seam in the rock. I waited until I heard her call out 'On belay!' and then, sending a quick prayer skyward, I started up the craggy granite. I made a point of not looking down.

I was starting to get the rhythm of it, when my foot slipped, and I felt myself starting to fall. My fingers dug into the slippery rock, struggling for a hold, and my right leg shot out, scrambling wildly for the ledge. Finally, my toe took hold, and I managed to pull myself back onto the rock. Unfortunately, I realized, I'd gotten myself into the dreaded spread-eagle position.

Maggie hadn't told me what to do if this happened. She'd just said not to let it happen. But it had. Okay, Cassidy, I told myself. You can't move forward without letting go with one limb. My left hand had the best grip but was already stretched as far as it would go. My right hand had a tenuous hold in a tiny crack, but if I let go with that hand, I wasn't sure my feet could hold me. Maybe if I could get my left foot up a little higher, into a larger groove, I'd be able then to move my right hand. The problem was, I was hugging the face of the rock so closely that I couldn't see if there were any cracks to be found. Well, that's what the damn rope is for, I thought grimly. One thing was certain. I couldn't just stay where I was. My legs and hands were starting to cramp.

Slowly, gripping as hard as I could with the other three points, I raised my left leg and sought a foothold. When my toe wedged into what felt like a good-sized crack, I nearly cried with joy. I was then able to bring my right hand over, find a better handhold, and from there resume my climb. When I reached Maggie, she was grinning like a fool.

"Not bad for a novice," she said as I collapsed onto the rock beside her.

"Jeez! Whose stupid idea was this, anyway?" I said, panting. I'd never worked so hard in my life.

"You're doing fine," she said. "We'll just repeat the process. See that next ledge?"

I didn't, but nodded anyway.

"Come on, let's coil these ropes, and get going." I think she was enjoying the fact that I wasn't as cocky as when we'd started. If and when we ever made it down this mountain, I promised myself, I'd take Ms. Maggie horseback riding. Sheriff Booker had a two-year-old mustang with a real penchant for bucking that ought to suit her just fine.

By the time we made it to the top of the ridge, I was soaked with sweat and my fingers were bleeding, but I felt strangely exhilarated. Maggie was beaming at me like a proud mother whose baby has just used the potty chair for the first time. I couldn't help it though. I was pretty proud of myself too.

"Okay," I whispered, once I'd caught my breath. "You stay here and lay low. I shouldn't be too long."

"I'm coming with you," she said. "There's no way you'll be able to find this exact spot in the dark. We may have to go down from another spot. We need to stick together."

This wasn't in the plan, but she was right. Once I left this spot, there was no way to ensure I'd be able to find it again.

"Okay," I said reluctantly. "Just stay close and keep down." I wasn't happy about this change in plans. It would be twice as hard to move quietly with two of us. But there was no point arguing about it. We were here, we may as well get started.

I stayed close to the trees, moving from one giant cedar to the next. Maggie followed suit, waiting for me to stop and listen before moving in behind me. It was slow going and the crunch of twigs beneath our feet seemed deafening at times, making my heart beat unnaturally fast. Now and then I heard a twig crackle up ahead of us and I'd strain to listen, only to decide it must have been a small rodent or bird. These woods, I knew, were full of all sorts of creatures and I preferred not to think about what we might run across in the dark.

We'd gone about six hundred yards when we heard a hissing sound, followed by a loud crack and a sudden shriek. There were footsteps, not fifty feet away, and Maggie and I froze, holding our breaths, hiding behind a tree. There were rustling noises, and then absolutely nothing. I strained to listen, afraid to breathe, but the night had gone silent.

"What do you think that was?" Maggie whispered so softly that I could barely hear her. I touched my finger to her lips and shook my head. I had no idea. We stood there for what seemed an eternity, eyes straining against the dark. Finally I decided to move. We could either go back or go forward, but we couldn't stand there forever. I took one tentative step and then another, gaining confidence when no sound was made. Slowly, we began inching forward.

Suddenly, not twenty feet away, I sensed a movement. I turned to signal Maggie to stay put, but she'd already started toward the next tree. I turned back and saw a figure emerge, and with the faint light of the moon, I could just make out the form of a man, dressed in army fatigues, raising his hand toward Maggie. Sound exploded in a hiss from the end of his outstretched hand, and there was a distinct thwack as Maggie was spun around and slammed to the ground. The figure raced toward her and was about to fall upon her when I leaped.

Still in midair, I caught him squarely on the chin with my foot, and I heard his neck snap back. His eyes were wild with surprise. He hadn't seen me coming. I took my revolver from the holster and grabbing the barrel, I swung as hard as I could. The metal handle of my gun met his skull with a sickening thud, and he fell to the ground.

Maggie's shirt was already soaked through with red, the sticky ooze spreading across her chest. Her eyes were wide with terror, and she held her hand to her chest where she'd been struck. It was very close to her heart.

I heard myself choke back a sob and leaned over to whisper in her ear. "I'll get you out of here. Don't worry." I was fighting tears. "Let me carry you."

"I think I can walk," she said, her voice trembling.

"Don't be silly," I whispered. I got my arms underneath her and started to lift.

"I'm serious," she said, sounding puzzled. "It hurts like hell, but I don't think it broke the skin."

"Hell, you've got blood all over you!" I hissed. But Maggie, resisting my attempts to pick her up, was struggling to show me something. She finally managed to lift her shirt, exposing her lovely breasts in the pale moonlight. They too were soaked with red, but when she wiped at them, there was no hole to be seen. Just an angry red and white welt. My mouth hung open stupidly.

"I think I was hit with a paint gun," she said, starting to giggle.

"A what?" I said, stunned. I rubbed some of the red with my fingers and sniffed them, verifying her guess. The relief washed over me with such force that I nearly collapsed. I'd thought Maggie was as good as dead. I looked at the form lying on the ground beside us. He wasn't moving. His eyes had rolled back in his head and his mouth hung open at a lopsided angle. I placed my finger to his neck and was relieved to find a faint but steady pulse. At least I hadn't killed him. And thank God I hadn't shot him!

I wondered suddenly how many others were out here in the dark, shooting at each other with paint guns. That thwack we'd heard earlier must have been another hit. Even as we sat there, I thought I heard a dull pop in the distance. We were smack in the middle of some stupid war game. Our chances of getting caught had just magnified tenfold.

"Come on," I said, helping Maggie to her feet. Despite her insistence that she was okay, I could tell she was shaken.

"Let's get out of here," I said. "Follow me, and stay low."

I started back the way we had come, but it soon became evident that we'd have to change course. The dull popping of paint bullets was growing louder, and we could hear people running all around us. Now and then, dark figures darted in and out from behind the trees, and at one point someone came so close to us that Maggie grabbed my hand and pulled me back.

"Maybe we should just stay here, wait for morning," she whispered.

Yeah, right, I thought. And at one o'clock Towne would call Martha and Booker, and everyone would be in a panic. Better to keep moving quietly and get our butts down the mountain as soon as possible.

"We'll be out of this soon," I told Maggie. "We're almost to the other side." I flashed her what I hoped was a confident, no-need-to-worry smile and headed off for the next tree, hoping I was right. The truth was, I had no idea where we were.

The sounds of the firing were growing more distant and we began to breathe easier. Another noise, like a faint humming, had been increasing, but I couldn't tell if it was made by insects or something mechanical. The trees were big enough and close enough together that we were under good cover, but at the same time there was very little light from the moon, so it was difficult to see. The ground had leveled out, and I suspected we were at the apex of the ridge. I wasn't entirely sure that we weren't going in circles. Suddenly, a shape loomed in front of us, and it took me a moment to realize that we had stumbled onto one of the canvas Quonset huts.

We pulled back, hiding behind a tree and studied the structure. It was different from the ones I'd seen earlier. It seemed to be smaller but it had a look of permanence. There was a rubber mat in front of the doorway, and with a start I realized there was a thin beam of light coming from inside. There was no way they could have strung electricity up this ridge. I had figured that the surveillance equipment was battery operated, but now it occurred to me that the humming I heard was some kind of generator, and it was nearby.

"Stay here," I said to Maggie. "I want to get a closer look."

"Come on, Cassie. Let's just go around." She didn't just sound worried, she sounded scared.

"I'll be right back," I said, ignoring her nervousness and my own trepidation.

I bent low to the ground and inched forward. One of the window flaps on the hut was open at the corner and I peered in, my heart racing. The room was mostly dark, but I immediately saw the source of light coming from inside. There were three separate monitors, each showing a darkened patch of ground. I recognized one as the path where Jessie and I had seen the first camera. To my relief, there didn't seem to be anyone monitoring the screens. I glanced back at Maggie, smiled just in case she could see my expression through the darkness, and stealthily made my way around to the front of the hut.

The door was just a zippered flap, like a big tent, and as quietly as I could, I unzipped it far enough to squeeze through. If there were someone inside, I'd know it in a second, because by now they'd have heard me. I crouched just inside the hut and listened.

Nothing. No sound of breathing, no rustling of clothing. I crept forward, one hand wrapped tightly around the butt of my gun, just in case.

The three monitors were set on a metal desk, and next to them was an IBM computer and laser printer. The computer screen was off, but I wondered what kind of work the Reverend did that required a computer way up here on the ridge. Clearly, this was the Reverend's personal hut. The black robe he'd worn in church was draped across the back of the single director's chair in front of the equipment. Electrical cords ran through a hole in the tent fabric to what I supposed was the generator out back. The rest of the room was divided into sleeping quarters, a makeshift bathroom, a small kitchenette and, along one wall, a bookshelf. I was curious to see what kind of books he read, but it was so dark in the room I couldn't make out the words. And more importantly, I wanted to get a look inside the locked metal drawers of his desk.

For once, I'd actually thought to bring the picks my old mentor Jake Parcell had given me. I selected by feel a small, eagle-nosed hook and inserted it into the tiny opening of the top right drawer. It took less than a minute to spring the minuscule lock. To my surprise, inside the drawer was another locked metal box. This lock was smaller than the first, and better made. It took me three tries before I heard the satisfying click that told me I'd broken in.

It was better than I'd hoped. Inside the box was a single computer disk. I slipped the disk into the pack around my waist and returned the locked box to the drawer which I relocked. With any luck, it would take Reverend Love a while to notice it was missing.

Pushing my luck, I opened one more drawer and found nothing more exciting than a thin booklet. It was impossible to make out the wording in the dark room, so I slipped it into my pack and relocked the drawer. I would have loved to stay longer, opening each drawer, poking around in the Reverend's belongings, but I had an uneasy feeling that I'd already overstayed my welcome.

I crept outside, squinting in all directions until I made out the tree where I'd left Maggie. She'd been right. Even without the men out there playing war games, it would have been nearly impossible to find the exact location where we'd come up the mountain. Just finding the right tree twenty feet away was difficult enough.

No sooner had I started to scurry over than a sharp voice shouted out across the blackness. "Halt! Who goes there?" It was the unmistakable booming baritone of the Reverend Love. Without thinking, I dove for the nearest tree and lay pressed against the sharp, rocky ground.

"You're out of the war zone," the Reverend's voice boomed. "Stand up and make yourself known. I repeat, you have strayed out of the zone. This is a command. Step forward." All the time he was speaking, he was walking toward me, and I could see his hands extended out in front of him, holding what looked like more than just a paint gun. I had no intention of stepping out to greet him.

Staying as low to the ground as possible, and keeping the trees between us, I dashed to the next tree, and then the next, my heart pounding so loud I couldn't tell if he was following or not. I had hoped to lead him away from Maggie, but I noticed with horror that she had joined me in jackrabbiting from tree to tree and was only ten yards behind me. I turned to tell her to go the other way, but as soon as I opened my mouth, I realized my mistake. The shot rang out, and a searing, blinding pain shot up through my left arm. Without thinking, I turned and fired back, my good hand shaking so badly that the shot caromed off a nearby tree. At this rate, I was more likely to hit Maggie than the Reverend.

I turned and ran again, ignoring the throbbing agony in my left arm. Another shot pierced the air, and the bullet whizzed so close to my ear that only my diving to the ground saved my head from being blown away. This time I could see him. The moon had broken through the trees and he was silhouetted against them, a dark, towering figure, not twenty feet away. I aimed my gun carefully, steadying my hand against a rock. I did not want to kill him. I was trespassing on his property. I had no right to be there, and he had every right to be shooting at me. If I killed him, it would be murder. But if I didn't do something, I'd be dead.

He was walking toward me, his gun extended. Sending up a silent prayer, I cocked the gun and fired. The sound of metal ripping into metal was nearly drowned out by his scream. I saw his gun arc into the air, white sparks lighting up the sky. It was a near-perfect shot, but by the sound of his scream, I was afraid I might have nicked a finger or two as well.

Not waiting to find out, I turned and ran full speed, catching up to Maggie and passing her. I could hear shouts in the distance, and I was sure the sounds of real gunfire would draw a crowd. There was nothing to do but run as fast as we could and hope to evade whatever pursuit they mounted. There was no doubt that once they saw that the Reverend had been shot, there would be dozens of men anxious to track us down.

We were both out of breath and gasping for air. My sides ached with the exertion, when we at last came to the edge of the ridge. It was not where we'd come up, but it was at least on the same side. We fell to the ground and were trying to catch our breath when Maggie noticed my arm.

"You've been shot!" she said. The look on her face made me glance down, and I noticed with horror that I had almost as much red on me as she did on her. Mine, however, was blood.

"I think it looks worse than it is," I said, feeling a surge of fear. What if I couldn't get down the mountain? Tentatively I opened and shut my left fist and extended my arm upward until I winced. It wasn't pleasant, but I thought I could make it work well enough to grasp the rope.

Maggie had taken off her backpack and was hurriedly searching for something. She pulled out a roll of gauze and ordered me to lift up my shirt.

"This is no time to get fresh," I said, wincing at the pain of lifting my arm.

"You wish," she said, helping me to peel off my jacket and shirt. The shirtsleeve had already stuck to the wound, and I had to grit my teeth and look away. I heard Maggie take in a deep breath, but her movements were quick and deft, and in no time, she'd managed to wrap the entire gauze bandage around my biceps. "Can you put this back on?"

"Just rip off the sleeve," I said. The bullet had

left a neat little puncture in the sleeve, and Maggie stuck her fingers in the hole and ripped away. Even without the sleeve, putting on the shirt wasn't easy.

"This is going to be a lot easier than coming up," she said. "Just take little hops, and keep yourself perpendicular to the rock. Use your legs, and if you need to rest, you can stop anytime you want."

Now, I thought. I'd really like to rest right now.

"I'm ready when you are," I lied.

Maggie leaned over, kissed me once on the lips and turned to pound a piton into the hard, craggy ground.

She was right. The first step was the toughest. I turned my back to the cliff, grabbed the rope with both hands, and stepped backwards into thin air. For a brief but terrifying moment, I thought I might plunge five hundred feet to my death. But my feet touched rock, and I was able to steady the rope so that by the time I took my third or fourth little hop, I was a lot less jerky and making what seemed to me a miraculously smooth descent. When I touched bottom, my knees went weak with relief.

Maggie was down a few moments later and began stuffing ropes back into her pack.

"Okay, Sherlock." She demanded, "I got you down. Now you get us back to Rick and Towne's."

With a pang, I realized that "Sherlock" was what Erica had called me too. But there was no time to dwell on Erica. We still had a long hike ahead of us.

The best I could figure, we were in easy walking distance to their house, except for the fact that there was no good place to walk. The shore was rocky and there were logs and fallen tree limbs all over the place. It only took us a few steps to realize that we'd

155

be better off in the water. The problem was, I had just ripped off a computer disk that I did not want damaged.

"Obviously you were never a Girl Scout," Maggie teased. She opened her backpack and took out a black hip pack. It was a large water-resistant bag which had held the first aid equipment. "Put it in here," she said, dumping the first aid stuff into her backpack.

I slipped my gun, my picks, the pamphlet and the computer disk inside the bag, and Maggie strapped it around her waist. We tucked the rest of our equipment behind a large boulder, marked it with a small pile of rocks and waded out into the frigid water.

It was colder than I expected, but after the long run, the strenuous climb up and down the mountain, and the plain old fear, it felt good to have the water wash away the sweat and blood. Even my arm felt better in the numbing water, though I was forced to sidestroke my way along the shore. Maggie was able to swim much faster, and it was she who first saw the lights on shore. She waited for me to catch up and asked me what I thought.

"It's either Rick and Towne," I said, gasping for breath, "or the Reverend's thugs. Either way, I don't think I can swim much farther. Stay here with the disk. If it's the guys, I'll wave you up. If it's not, keep going."

"Cass, wait," she said, pulling me back. We were waist high in the water and my teeth had begun to chatter. She pulled me to her and slipped her arms around my waist. As she kissed me, a surge of warmth spread through my body. Better than brandy,

I thought. Despite my shaking, I didn't want to move. Finally, I pulled myself away and trudged up the bank toward the flashlights, hoping like hell it wasn't the Reverend waiting there.

"Cassidy?" Towne said. "Is that you?"

Relief flooded through me. I'd never been so glad to see anyone. I waved Maggie forward, and together we pulled ourselves up the rocky slope.

"Oh, my God!" Rick cried, seeing the red paint on the front of Maggie's wet shirt. The water had made it look even more like blood. "You're bleeding!" He looked like he might faint.

"I'm fine," Maggie said. "It's red paint. She's the one who's bleeding."

"Come on, let's get out of here," I said, shrugging off their concern. I didn't know how bad the wound was, but if I didn't get into some dry clothes soon, it would be a moot point, because I'd freeze to death. But the look on their faces told me the bleeding was far from over. We started forward, and I paused to look back up to the top of the ridge. There, high above us, I saw two tiny, moonlit figures huddled together, peering down at us through some kind of scope. Oh great, I thought. The Reverend was watching our every move. I hurried to catch up with the others, but I'd only taken a few steps before I felt my legs go weak beneath me. Before I knew what was happening, I felt the earth coming up to meet me, and my vision suddenly went black. I braced myself for the fall, felt myself falling and falling, but instead of the hard, rocky ground, it was Towne's arms catching me, lifting me up, cradling me all the way home.

When I opened my eyes, they were standing over

me, concern creasing their faces. I was propped up on a sofa, swathed in blankets, naked as a newborn. My arm throbbed miserably, but the shaking had subsided.

"You need to see a doctor," Towne said. "You've lost too much blood."

"I think I'm okay now," I said. In fact I was feeling rather light-headed.

"I've rewrapped your arm," Maggie said. "And I put in some butterfly stitches, but you're going to need some real stitches soon. The bullet passed right through, thank God."

"Do you think it will hold till morning?" I asked. "I think what I really need is some sleep."

"I think it will," Maggie said, "if you don't roll around too much. But we need to get some nourishment in you, to counteract the blood loss. Rick made you a cup of broth. Here."

I think they were enjoying bossing me around, but I was too tired to protest. I sipped the broth, and let them rearrange my pillows and blankets, fussing over me like three mother hens. Actually, it was kind of nice, I thought, feeling myself slip back down into a deep, bottomless slumber. I don't think I moved once all night.

Chapter Sixteen

I awoke with a stiff neck and a relentlessly throbbing arm. My mouth felt as if I'd been sucking on desert sand. But the sight of Rick, sound asleep in an easy chair across from me, made me smile. He'd apparently been assigned guard duty, and from the circles under his eyes, it looked as if he'd just recently succumbed to sleep. When I moved, his eyes shot open and he practically leaped out of his chair.

"You're up!" he said, happily. How anyone could be that cheerful upon waking was beyond me.

"What time is it?" I asked, squinting at the bright

light pouring in through the windows. It looked suspiciously like midday.

"It's after ten," Rick said. "You slept like a baby. Towne gave Maggie a ride into town. They both had to get to work. How's your arm?"

I had managed to push myself up off the couch and remembering my unclothed state, held one of the blankets around me. "It's pretty good," I lied. "Do you have any clothes I can borrow?"

"Yours are in the dryer. You can borrow a shirt though. I threw away that bloody rag you were wearing."

That bloody rag had been my favorite shirt. Oh well. I stumbled into the bathroom and examined my reflection with a grimace. My hair looked like something Don King would be proud of, but otherwise I looked no worse for the wear. The bandage Maggie had wrapped around my arm seemed to be doing the trick, and there was only the slightest sign of blood oozing through.

Gingerly, I pulled on one of Rick's flannel shirts, two sizes too big, but nice and soft. I patted down my hair with water and drank about five dixie cups of clean, cold water. I splashed some on my face, and squeezed toothpaste onto a finger which I rubbed around on my teeth. Declaring myself ready for the day, I finished dressing and joined Rick in the kitchen.

"Maggie says you should eat before I take you to the doctor." Rick set a large glass of orange juice on the table in front of me. "Sit here."

They were really taking this mothering thing to the hilt. But the truth was, I was famished and I made little protest as he served me toast and eggs — poached, no less — with two pieces of bacon and a cup of coffee with real cream. I devoured it all and had a second glass of orange juice. By the time I'd finished, I was feeling pretty frisky.

"About the doctor," I said, getting up to help clear the table. "I'm pretty sure I can manage that myself. Besides, there's something I need to do first."

"But Maggie said you should go in right away," he said, following me into the living room. There on the coffee table was the waterproof hip pack with the computer disk and my other belongings safely dry inside. I gathered it up along with my boat keys and turned to smile at Rick.

"I know," I said, reassuringly. "And I promise I'll go right in, as soon as I take care of this. But if I don't get going right now, I won't get there before noon. Besides," I said, "you look as if you could use a nap." I'd caught him stifling a yawn, and now he looked at me sheepishly and grinned.

"Okay," he said. "But call me as soon as you get back from the doctor. You are going to tell the sheriff about what you guys found up there last night, aren't you?" He walked me down the path to my boat. I assured him I would and pushed off, gunning it all the way into town.

I docked at the county dock, not wanting to take the extra time it took to go through the channel to the marina. A half-dozen people were lounging around the fishing dock, smoking and shooting the breeze. It was a warm, sunny day, and for a second I was tempted to join them. It had been a long time since I'd just spent an afternoon fishing off my dock, sipping beer. Maybe when this case was over, I thought, I'd have Maggie out to the house and we'd do just that.

It was only a ten-minute walk to the sheriff's office, but the previous night's adventures had caused aches and pains in muscles I didn't know I had, and I was feeling every one of them. When I got to the old brick building, I was disappointed to see the "closed" sign hung on the door. The sheriff's secretary was already out to lunch, and Booker had either decided to join her or was out doing sheriff stuff. I could page him on his beeper, but then I'd have to stand by a pay phone and wait for him to call. It was maddening that the rest of the world carried cell phones while Cedar Hills was still unable to use them. There were just too many hills and trees between the lake and the cellular service area. I could always track Booker down at one of the restaurants in town, provided that's where he was, but that could end up being a huge waste of time. What I really needed, I decided, was to get my hands on an IBM compatible PC.

I walked over to the county library hoping that they'd included one in their recent technological upgrades, but found that they'd only added another Macintosh to their arsenal. They now had three of them. And then I did what I knew I'd end up doing all along; I headed for the old Methodist Church.

The church was empty, and I could see dust motes floating lazily in the sunlight streaming through the windows. Tentatively, I made my way to the back door and peered through the one small window. There did not appear to be anyone inside. Even so, I decided it might be prudent to knock this time. When no one answered my third knock, I slipped out my handy picks and went to work on the locks. To my surprise, they had installed a dead bolt, which took me a little longer to master, but still, I was inside in a couple of minutes.

The room was as I remembered it, minus Herman Hugh. The IBM computer sat on the old wooden desk, and I slipped into the creaky wooden teacher's chair and got to work. The computer hummed to life with a switch and the screen blinked on, asking for a password.

"Damn," I mumbled. I hadn't counted on this. Well, I had nothing to lose, I thought. So I started typing in possible passwords, hitting return and waiting for the screen to tell me "Invalid Entry." I typed in "Reverend," "Reverend Love" and "Love." I got the same answer every time. I tried "Herman," "H Hugh" and "Pittman," with the same results. I tried "KKK," "Christian" and "Loveland." I wished I could remember all the subsidiary names Martha had told me, but my mind was drawing a blank. When I'd tried everything I could think of, out of frustration I typed in the "F" word and laughed at myself for halfway expecting it to do the trick.

Admitting defeat, I slipped the disk back into the hippack, and noticed the pamphlet I'd taken from the Reverend's desk drawer. Curious, I picked it up and was surprised by the title: "West Coast Militia: The Final Plan."

I flipped through the pages and felt myself growing ill. The pages were filled with hate-inspired rhetoric, racist propaganda and gross illustrations. One page was titled, "The Ten Best Ways To Kill A Jew." The message throughout the pamphlet was clear. The government was the enemy, and it had to be stopped.

Where had this mentality come from, I wondered. I thought of Ruby Ridge, Waco and even the Unabomber. How many of these weirdos were out there? I thought of the Reverend's churches and his retreats. Those guys weren't just up there playing paintball war games. Love was using the ridge as a training ground for anti-government activities. Even his church sermon made quite a few references to the "army of Love." Obviously, he was recruiting soldiers for his militia. And from the filth I'd just read, I knew it wasn't just the government these people intended to attack.

My hands felt dirty just from touching the pages and I stuffed the pamphlet back into the pack. Then, in what must have been a moment of inspiration, or complete luck, I retrieved the disk and slipped it back into the slot. I typed in "Final Plan," and was rewarded with a series of clicks and hums and a rapidly filling screen.

I flicked on the printer, waited for it to warm up, and selected "Print" from the file menu. The whirring sound filled the room as page after page of indecipherable numbers and letters shot out of the printer, into my waiting hands. There were nearly twenty pages all together, and I carefully tucked them into my pack, along with the disk, before turning the computer off. I was halfway to the door, when I heard a key in the lock.

I leaped back behind the desk and crouched beneath it just before the door swung open. I hadn't thought to relock the door, and now whoever had tried their key probably knew someone had been inside. I peered out from underneath the desk, my heart pounding, and saw the pinched, imperious face of Herman Hugh. He was eyeing the room, his hands on his hips. The freckles that dotted his face stood out against his alabaster skin like angry welts. As he looked toward the desk, his eyes became pale slits.

He moved toward the desk, and my heart pounded. I held my breath. He stood on the other side of the desk, looking down at the printer, and I suddenly realized that I hadn't turned the printer off! Herman Hugh marched around the desk, his feet inches from my face. If he looked down, he'd see me, crouched like a coward beneath the desk. I didn't want to get caught by Herman Hugh. Besides, my legs were starting to cramp. If I didn't move soon, I wasn't sure I'd be able to. When I heard him slide the desk drawer open, I remembered his gun and decided the time had come to move.

Hoping for the best, I kicked out with my right leg and caught Herman Hugh squarely on the knee-cap. His leg buckled, and I made the same kick at his other leg, sending him sprawling. I raced out from under the desk. The gun had fallen to the floor between us. I picked it up and saw his pale eyes grow wide with fear. I stood over him, watching him cower, obviously in pain. If I had some rope, I thought, I could tie him up. But there wasn't exactly time to search the room. So I did what had worked so nicely the night before. Grabbing the gun by the barrel, I took a mighty back swing and conked him on his pointy little skull. He was out instantly.

"You're getting pretty good at that," I said out loud, hoping I hadn't hit him too hard. People died of head wounds, I told myself, hurrying out the door.

Maybe I should have checked his pulse, but I was in a hurry to get in touch with the sheriff. Whatever the Reverend was up to, it was serious enough that he'd found it necessary to use some kind of secret code on his own disk. I only hoped that I'd be smart enough to break it.

Chapter Seventeen

The first thing I did was call both Martha and Booker from the pay phone outside the library. As luck would have it, I had to leave a message for each of them. My message was short and sweet.

"This is Cass. I'm at the county library. I'm in possession of something I think you should see right away. Meet me here immediately. It's twelve-thirty." I knew Martha checked in for her messages on the hour, and Doris, the sheriff's secretary should be returning from lunch soon. She'd know how to get in touch with the sheriff, and for now, that was the best I could do.

I went inside the small library and headed for a table in the back. There wasn't another soul in the place, except for Mrs. Peters, the librarian, who waved at me when I entered. I spread all twenty pages out on the table and began to examine them. Each page was empty except for a single line of numbers and letters across the top. It took me forever to recognize a pattern.

The first group of numbers on each page had six digits and ended with 96. Once I saw that similarity, I figured out that the first group of numbers on each page indicated a date. I decided to concentrate on the top page and see what else I could decipher. The top page looked like this:

060196 — 1400 — 47N 122W — 19 16 1 3 5 /14
5 5 4 12 5 — 7 15 18 5 — 3 1 12/ 2 15 13 2

Beneath 060196 I wrote June 1, 96. I figured 1400 could easily be 2:00, so I had the date and time, but of what? The next numbers had N and W by them, which might stand for North and West. Suddenly I had an idea, and I called over to Mrs. Peters. She was a pink, plump lady with hair so white it looked blue. She was wearing a flowered print shift and white support hose that matched her hair.

"Did you need help, dear?" she asked, showing me her pearly dentures.

"Mrs. Peters, if you saw these numbers by themselves, what would you think they might mean?"

I showed her the 47N 122W. She peered at them through her half-glasses and frowned.

"My first guess would be degrees of latitude and longitude," she said. When I looked at her blankly, she walked over to her desk and came back with a globe. "You can find anywhere on earth by using degrees of latitude and longitude," she explained. "Latitude always comes first. Let's see." She began tracing her finger along the globe until she came to the spot where the two points intersected. "There! You see? Forty-seven degrees north and one hundred and twenty-two degrees west is Seattle!" The look of triumph on her face was beatific.

"Would you mind figuring out a few more for me?" I asked, getting excited. I showed her the other pages and in each case, the third grouping contained degrees of latitude and longitude. Mrs. Peters went right to work, and while she began writing in the names of cities, I tried to decipher the next set of numbers.

The highest number in the group was nineteen. I checked the other pages, and in no case was there a number higher than twenty-six. There are twenty-six letters in the alphabet, I thought, wondering if it could be that simple.

I started with the simplest possibility, letting A equal 1, B equal 2 and so on. I didn't expect it to work, but to my surprise, it did. For some reason, the Reverend had thought a code was necessary, but he clearly never really expected anyone to stumble upon the disk, or he would have made it more difficult.

In just over a minute, I had the last three

groupings deciphered, and what I read sent shivers down my spine. It read, SPACE NEEDLE —GORE — CAR BOMB.

The sound of the library door opening caused both Mrs. Peters and me to jump. It was Martha, looking worried. She was in uniform, and I thought she looked particularly cute, despite the concern on her face. I waved her over and thanked Mrs. Peters, asking if she'd leave us alone for a moment. She looked disappointed, but I assured her she'd been a huge help. When she left, I filled Martha in on what I'd found up on the ridge, and the fact that I'd stolen the Reverend's disk. When I told her about the war games, her eyes widened.

"You went up there alone?" she asked.

"Uh, no." I said, squirming. "I took Maggie Carradine. She's an experienced rock climber," I added hastily. Martha's eyes were huge.

"You went with Doctor Carradine? I didn't even know you knew each other!" I could see her calculating the possibilities. "When did you meet?" she asked. It was just like Martha to get side-tracked.

"At the dinner dance you took me to," I said, smiling sheepishly.

"Oh ho!" Martha said. "I should have known!" Her eyes were beaming. "Why didn't you tell me?" she asked, suddenly looking hurt.

"Uh, Martha. Do you think we could get back to the matter at hand? This *is* kind of important." She nodded but had trouble keeping the grin off her face.

I showed her the first completed page, and her face suddenly became serious.

"Jesus, Cass. This looks like an assassination plot. June first is only three days away!" She looked down at the other pages, and shook her head. Mrs. Peters had figured out the next three locations which included San Diego, Atlanta and Chicago. I looked quickly at the dates on the other pages, and noticed they were in chronological order. Over the course of the next year the West Coast Militia planned at least twenty incidents.

"You know what's happening the last week in July in Atlanta," I said.

"The olympics," Martha said. "And look, the Republican convention is in San Diego this year, in August." I showed Martha the alphabet code, and as quickly as we could, we began filling in the letters. It didn't take us long to realize that each page contained the name of a prominent government leader, detailing the location and manner in which he or she was to be assassinated.

"We need to verify that these people have plans to be in those places on those dates." Martha said, moving quickly toward Mrs. Peters's desk.

The door swung open, and Sheriff Booker came in, looking out of breath. "This better be good," he grumbled. "The lodge is serving chicken-fried steak." When I didn't laugh, he hurried over and I filled him in. Booker was a better listener than Martha and didn't interrupt once. By the time I'd finished, Martha was back.

"Seattle Chamber of Commerce confirms that the Vice President is scheduled to tour their city June first, and guess what? The Space Needle is one of the stops."

"Holy shit," Booker said. "How many men do you think you saw up there, Cass?"

"I saw enough sleeping bags for maybe twenty or

thirty men," I said. "But that was only in one hut. There were other huts up there. One was like a mess hall, and another had duffel bags that might have contained some kind of weapons."

"They can't all be involved in these assassination plots," Martha said.

"For all we know, the Reverend really does run a retreat. Those men might be up there playing war games, completely unaware that their leader is planning the real thing down below." Booker ran a hand through his silver hair. "I think we should alert the FBI on this."

"I've already called Captain Tell," Martha said. "He's on his way over now. He's hesitant to call in the Feds until he's seen the evidence himself."

"We don't have time for that!" Booker said, sounding disgusted. "The fact that the Reverend saw Cass up there last night probably means he won't be staying long. We need the FBI in here now. I'm not going to wait around for Tell." He was already moving toward the phone.

"There's only one path down that mountain," I said. "Unless they come down on ropes like we did, they'll use the old Scout path. Someone should watch that area." Booker was nodding, reaching for the phone.

"As soon as I get through to the FBI, I'll be over there myself," he said, starting to dial. I turned to Martha, who was gathering up the papers.

"I'll need the disk, too," she said. I retrieved it from the pack, and saw Martha's eyes take in the gun.

"I, uh, might have accidentally shot off a couple

of the Reverend's fingers," I said. "I was aiming at his gun, but he did let out a little scream, so . . ."

Martha was shaking her head. "If I'd have known you'd end up being such a damned hero, I'd never have talked you into becoming a private eye in the first place," she said. I think she was actually more ticked off about my not telling her about Maggie, but even so, I was glad I hadn't told her about the hole in my arm. So far, I'd managed to do everything one-handed, and as far as I knew, it hadn't bled any more.

"I've got to meet the captain over at the county court house," she went on rather curtly. "He should be there any minute. He may want to talk to you later, so please go home and stay by the phone."

"Why can't I just come with you now?" I asked, sounding like a little kid.

"You don't know him, Cass. Trust me. He hates private investigators. It's better this way. Please, just this once, do as I say."

Okay, fine, I thought. Martha, who never could stay mad for long, saw that I was pouting and put her arm around my shoulder, walking me to the door. Luckily she didn't see me wince at the pain she had inadvertently caused.

"You did good, babe," she said. She squeezed my arm affectionately, bringing tears of agony to my eyes, and rushed out to the police car she'd parked halfway up on the curb. Booker came out a moment later and headed for his own car.

"The damn fools won't be here for an hour," he said. "By then, they could all be gone. What's wrong with your arm?"

"Uh, nothing," I said, holding it gingerly where Martha had squeezed it. "Tom?" I said.

He stopped, mid-stride and looked at me questioningly.

"It could be that one of them, at least, is right around the corner at the church. I kind of conked Herman Hugh on the head a little while ago. Last I saw him, he was sawing off some pretty serious Z's."

"Well, why in hell didn't you say so sooner!" he yelled. He slammed his car door, and took off toward the church, throwing loose gravel off his tires as he went.

For some reason, I felt totally depressed. It was like, Gee, thanks for all your help, Cass. Now go home. Sure, you singlehandedly saved the world. So what? Still babying my arm, I mumbled these and other equally self-pitying thoughts all the way back to the county dock.

I was halfway home when I remembered Mrs. Larsen's telescope. It was a high-powered scope with both short- and long-range capabilities. I hadn't tried it on anything but the houses across the way but I imagined it could also be used to see the top of the ridge. I turned my boat in a wide arc, and jetted full-speed to her dilapidated old dock.

This time, she came out to greet me, seeming almost cheerful. She was wearing a tiny lime-green house-dress and had smeared some matching eye-shadow above her lids in an attempt to liven up her pale face. Her watery eyes were yellowish pink where the whites should have been, but she looked better than the last time I'd seen her.

"He passed on last night," she informed me as I

came up the rickety stairway to her house. "They came and took him away less than an hour ago."

"I'm terribly sorry," I said, thinking that this hadn't been such a hot idea after all.

"Well, you can be as sorry as you want, but I, for one, am relieved." I followed her into the house and noticed that she had made an honest effort to clean up. She'd even opened the windows, and the place smelled a little better too.

"Still," I said, "I know how hard it must have been, having someone you love dying. It takes a while to get over something like that."

She snorted and retrieved a partially full glass off the counter before leading me into the living room. "Not that someone your age would know anything about it," she said.

I didn't feel like telling her about Diane, who had suffered terribly before finally giving into the cancer that consumed her body. I didn't feel like telling her I knew what it was like to actually feel relieved when she was finally out of her pain. And even if I had told her, I didn't think she really wanted to hear it.

"So, did you bring it?" she asked, hoisting herself up onto the sofa. When I looked at her blankly, she added, "The Cutty Sark. You said you'd bring me a bottle."

"Uh, no. Sorry. I came to borrow your telescope. You don't mind if I take a peek do you?"

She looked incredulous, then crestfallen. She'd been sure I'd come equipped with her specified bribe. I almost felt sorry that I hadn't thought of it, even though the last thing Mrs. Larsen seemed to need was another bottle of booze. I crouched down to look through the lens and noticed that she'd refocused it back on Rick and Towne's bedroom. Scowling, I started to swing it upward toward the top of the ridge, when something caught my eye. Slowly, I brought the scope back toward the house, wondering what it was I'd seen that seemed out of place. And there it was. The blinds were closed. Not just the ones in the bedroom, but all of them. They'd been wide open that morning, and I couldn't for the life of me think of one good reason why Rick would suddenly close them.

And then, with a start, I flashed on the image I'd seen the night before, just before I'd passed out. High up on the top of the ridge, I'd seen two figures huddled over binoculars, peering down at the four of us heading back to Rick and Towne's. Which meant that they knew where we had gone. Which meant that Rick could be in danger. Because if the Reverend had discovered his disk was missing, he might just decide to come looking for it.

Without another word to the startled Mrs. Larsen, I flew out of the house, down the rickety steps and into my boat, gunning the engine all the way over to Rick and Towne's.

Chapter Eighteen

The minute I climbed the stairs to their house, I knew something was wrong. Not only were the blinds all drawn, but the sliding glass door was partially open, as if someone had not taken the time to close it properly. I reached into the hip pack I still wore and took out my gun. Maybe I was overreacting, I told myself. Maybe Rick was trying to catch up on his sleep, and had pulled the shades. But the hammering in my chest did not subside.

I squeezed through the open door as silently as I could and nearly gagged. Someone had taken a knife and slashed to shreds every single painting on the wall. Rick's beautiful paintings had been savaged. I stood stock still and listened to the silent house, straining to hear any sounds over the pounding of my heart.

"Tell me where!" a familiar voice boomed. "I'm giving you just one more chance!"

I heard what must have been another painting being stabbed and ripped, and I tiptoed forward toward the den to peek through the doorway. The Reverend's back was to me, and I watched dumbfounded as he slashed away at Rick's last painting with a knife. In the corner, his eyes closed, as if refusing to witness the last of his paintings destroyed, was Rick. His hands were tied behind his back, and he dangled, suspended from a wooden ceiling beam by a noose around his neck. His toes just barely touched the carpet.

"Now where is she, you little faggot?" the Reverend shouted, turning toward Rick, his eyes black with fury. Rick opened his eyes, but kept silent. Reverend Love walked over to him with the knife, and held it against his throat. A tiny line of red popped to the surface and began to trickle down Rick's throat. Still, he said nothing.

"I'm right here," I said, cocking my gun and stepping into the room. The Reverend wheeled around so fast he nearly lost his balance.

"Drop the knife, Reverend," I said. He smiled then, and I wondered why I'd never noticed the yellowing teeth. There was an odd stench coming off him. Apparently he'd worked up quite a sweat ripping up Rick's paintings. With hardly a pang of guilt, I noticed his right hand was heavily bandaged around the last two fingers. He held the knife gingerly with the other three.

"Where is the pamphlet?" he said, spitting out each syllable.

"Put down the knife and we'll talk about it," I said with a calm that surprised me. Rick's eyes had gone wide with fear. He seemed more afraid for me than he had for himself. I took a step closer to the Reverend and aimed the gun squarely between his eyes. Slowly he set the knife on the floor.

"Kick it away," I said. I could see he didn't like taking orders, but his knife was no match for my gun.

"There," he said, "Now hand over the pamphlet and I'll be on my way."

Was he bluffing me? Or did he not know I had the disk?

"It's too late, Reverend. The FBI has it now. Along with the disk. And they know all about your assassination plans, starting with the car bomb at the Space Needle in Seattle on June first when the Vice President will be visiting."

His eyes narrowed and his mouth opened and closed. Then he laughed. "I don't know what you're talking about."

"Sure you do, Reverend. Or should I call you Alex?"

This time he couldn't conceal his surprise.

"That's right. I know all about McCall, Idaho, Portland and the rest." Which wasn't entirely true, but what the hell? I went on. "All those phony churches were just a way to recruit men into your militia. And I know why you blackmailed the people on Cedar Ridge, too. You couldn't afford to have them see or hear what you were doing on the top of the ridge. It's not just war games you're playing up there, is it Rev? You really believe all that crap in those pamphlets, don't you? And you work on others until they believe it too."

His eyes had grown more menacing as I spoke, but I couldn't seem to stop myself. "You've got little pockets of extremists all over this country, just waiting for you to sound the alarm. Isn't that right, Rev? And then what? You planning on killing us all?"

By now his eyes had grown so dark and narrow that he regarded me through pupilless, snake-like slits. "You can't prove any of this," he said, his voice uncharacteristically low. He took a step toward me but I raised the gun and he stopped.

"The FBI have the ridge surrounded right now," I lied. "Your men will all be arrested." This time, his laugh was loud. More like a growl than a laugh, I thought. It scared me.

"My soldiers have been gone for over ten hours," he said. "There's not one shred of evidence left of our having been up there. Evacuation drills are the first thing we practice. I only came back for the pamphlet, but now that I see that it's pointless, I'll be on my way."

"What about the disk?" I asked.

"What fucking disk?" he barked. "I don't know a damned thing about any disk!"

The way his voice had risen, it occurred to me that he might be telling the truth. But how could he be?

"I took it out of your drawer, right below the computer. I broke the code. The FBI has it now. The whole plan is off." As I spoke, I saw his gaze shift behind me. I'd fallen for this kind of trick before. He wanted me to turn around so he could jump me. I didn't budge.

"She's right, you know." The voice came so suddenly, I jumped.

Herman Hugh was standing in the doorway, his gun leveled at my head.

"What the hell is she talking about?" the Reverend roared. But for the first time, I thought I saw more than crazy hatred in his eyes. I saw fear.

"She's talking about the real plan, Alex. Not those pathetic games you play. You didn't really think the movement was going to rely on a bunch of misfits and rednecks with rifles?"

"How dare you speak to me that way!" The Reverend's dark face had become mottled with rage.

"Actually, Alex, I've grown rather weary of speaking to you altogether. You weren't to know of our plans. You're considered something of a security risk. But you have proven yourself handy at times. Heaven knows when we might have to actually use some of your recruits. You've done a fine job getting them in place. Unfortunately, your usefulness has come to an end." The freckles dotting Herman Hugh's pale complexion stood out like hills on a relief map. His grin was condescending.

"Toss your gun, detective." The last word dripped with sarcasm as he trained the barrel of his gun on Rick. Slowly, I set the gun on the floor and kicked it away.

"You've ruined everything!" the Reverend bellowed. Before I knew what was happening, he dove across the room at Herman Hugh.

The sound of a single gunshot split the air and

Reverend Love's body jerked backward before slumping to the ground.

"You always thought I was second fiddle," Herman said, toeing the Reverend's inert body. "I guess now you know."

I knew it was the only chance I'd get, even if it wasn't a very good one. Before he could turn his gun on me, I dove. I caught him waist-high and he tumbled backward with me on top of him. I heard his head hit the floor but before I could take advantage of my position, I also heard the metallic click of the gun's hammer.

"You're dead," he said.

"Not yet," I said, rolling to the right and kicking as hard as I could. I caught his chin with my heel. This time the sound was more like the snapping of brittle kindling.

A shot fired out, ricocheting against the far wall, and I leaped on top of him, pounding his wrist against the floor until he was forced to release the gun. I shoved it away, but when I did, his right fist slammed into my jaw, sending me sprawling. He lunged before I could regroup, and I felt his sharp fingernails rake my cheek, drawing blood from my temple to my chin. I bunched up my right fist and, putting my weight behind it, punched him in the belly as hard as I could. He doubled over, gasping.

Before he could recover, I hit him again, this time in the face, and his nose burst open with blood. He came at me then with a vengeance. He was all arms and legs, swinging wildly, connecting a lot. He had no interest in the gun now. He wanted to kill me with his bare hands. He caught me by the hair and yanked out a fistful. I kicked him in the crotch, causing him to double over again, yowling like an enraged bull. He grabbed hold of my earring, and yanked downward, ripping my earlobe in two. I could feel the warm trickle of blood seep down my neck.

I went for his knees then, knowing they'd be sore from where I'd kicked him before, but he grabbed my leg and flipped me upside down. Rick was yelling for me to get up, but I let Herman Hugh come at me, knowing something he didn't. This was one of the first self-defense moves I'd learned. Bending over me, he was not in a position of strength, and I was. I used both legs, kicked straight up into Herman Hugh's face, and knocked him backward. I followed with a solid right to the gut, and when he doubled over, I finally got two good kicks to the knees and a solid kick to his chin which snapped his neck back and made the whites of his eyes roll upward. He went down like a wet dishrag.

I stood over him, waiting for him to get up so I could kick him again. I wasn't proud of this sudden taste for violence, but I couldn't help it. I was almost disappointed to realize Herman Hugh had decided to take another siesta. With trembling legs, I went over to where the Reverend lay in a dark pool of blood and needlessly checked his pulse. Whatever measly soul he may have once possessed had already fled to parts beyond.

Rick's eyes were filled with tears. He had the look of someone who had accepted his own death and then been given an unexpected reprieve, as if he'd passed into some other, more elevated state of being. He looked at me as if he didn't quite understand what all the fuss was about. Gingerly, I loosened the noose around his neck and helped him down, untying the rope around his wrists as well. Neither of us seemed able to speak.

I used the rope to tie up Herman Hugh and then went into the kitchen to call the sheriff's office. My voice sounded funny, talking through puffed and broken lips, but I managed to get the pertinent information across. Rick went into the bathroom and came out with some wet rags, which he proceeded to use on my face while I talked on the phone. I was surprised at the amount of blood that came away, and when I looked down at my arm, I realized that it too had begun to bleed again in earnest. I wasn't really feeling the pain though. My arm had gone temporarily numb. All I felt was the devastating loss of Rick's artwork, like an impenetrable lump of rubber in my throat.

We sat together out on the front deck overlooking the lake, holding hands. He'd brought me a beer, and I took dainty little sips out of one side of my mouth, alternately holding it against my left eye, which had started to close. I had never sat so long with another person, saying nothing. It had never been necessary. When at last I saw the sheriff's orange and white boat round the tip of the peninsula, I felt a pang of regret. Soon this temporary state of grace we had entered would be shattered. There would be words, and action, and pain. Rick squeezed my hand, as if he read my mind.

Behind Booker's boat came another and another. Uniformed cops, including Martha, swarmed the dock. With a deep sigh, I got up to greet them.

Chapter Nineteen

The best parties are sometimes totally impromptu. It was only four days after Herman Hugh and I had made mincemeat of each other's faces, and somehow Martha and Rick had managed to organize a Sunday get-together at my place. They thought I needed cheering up, but in truth, I didn't feel nearly as bad as I looked. I'd had my ear sewn back together and a dozen stitches put in my arm, so mostly it was just the bluish-green tint to my face that had people worried. I had four perfect claw marks running from my left temple to my chin, which despite constant applications of Neosporin, had festered. And my left eye had a good old-fashioned shiner. But other than that, I was feeling pretty good. It was Rick I was worried about. As far as I knew, he hadn't even started to deal with the loss of his paintings. Outwardly he seemed fine, but his eyes reflected a sadness that worried me.

We were out back, where Booker had set up the horseshoes, and Jess Martin was tending a makeshift bar in the unfinished greenhouse. Martha and Tina were beating the pants off Booker and his wife, Rosie, at horseshoes, and Rick, who'd insisted on doing all the cooking, was playing the role of hostess, seeming to love every minute of it. They were all taking turns waiting on me, and I'd be a liar if I said I wasn't milking it for all it was worth.

Maggie was the most solicitous of all. She kept reaching up to touch my face, grimacing with concern, and each time she did, my stomach somersaulted, and a warm glow spread through me. As much as I was enjoying everyone's company, I couldn't wait to have Maggie all to myself.

Towne was teaching little Jessie to play darts and Lizzie Thompson had made it her personal mission to refill Martha's plate and drink every time Rick came around with a new hors d'oeuvre. Tina was beginning to give Lizzie cold looks, but Martha was basking in the attention. She may have been totally smitten with Tina, but it was in her nature to flirt, and asking her not to was like asking Panic not to catch mice.

Speaking of which, both Panic and Gammon had taken to birddogging Rick, and I suspected he was feeding them little morsels of the wonderful pâtés and salmon tarts he'd just brought out. Either that, or somehow, with their superior feline sensitivity, they understood that Rick was hurting inside.

When the doorbell rang, I got up to see who else could possibly have been invited to this little shindig.

She stood in the doorway, her blue eyes more beautiful than I remembered. The California sun had baked her skin so brown she looked exotic, and her smile exposed the perfect white teeth that I remembered.

"Erica," I said, finally forcing my mouth to work.

"My God, what happened to you?" She reached out and touched my face, and I winced, not at the pain, but at the sudden jolt of electricity that ran through me.

"You look terrible," she said, moving her hand.

I backed up nervously, and tried a chuckle. "Thanks a lot," I said. "You look, uh, really great." This was no lie.

"You like my hair?" she asked. She turned so I could see the new cut and I had to admit, I did like it. Erica had the kind of hair that would look good no matter what she did to it, but the way it was layered back, the nearly black, shiny waves framed her oval face, accentuating those startling blue eyes. While I pretended to study her hair, I was intensely aware of her body. She was wearing a royal blue pullover sleeveless sweatshirt made of some soft, rich material that made me want to run my hands over her breasts. My mouth had gone completely dry and when I looked up at her again, she laughed.

187

"Oh, Cassidy," she said, moving closer. "God, I've missed you." She stepped toward me and took me in her arms. It was just a hug, I told myself, trying to ignore her breasts pressed against my own. My heart had begun to hammer inside my chest and while my mouth had gone dry, other parts of my body were far from it.

"Hello." The voice came from behind us, startling us both, and I pulled guiltily away. Maggie was standing in the hallway, holding my wine glass and hers.

"Uh, Maggie, this is a friend of mine, Erica Trinidad," I said, feeling the blush spread across my bruised cheeks. I hoped the blue and green would mask the new color but I doubted it. "Erica, this is Doctor Maggie Carradine," I said. Why I had thrown in her title, I had no idea.

"A doctor, huh? It looks like Cass could use one." Erica looked from Maggie to me and back again. "Glad to meet you," she added belatedly. I'd have given anything just then to be out back playing horseshoes with Martha.

"Actually, I'm a psychologist. I'd shake your hand, but..." Maggie held up the two glasses apologetically.

Erica laughed. "It's okay, I've always thought handshaking was overrated anyway. Personally, I prefer hugging."

"So I noticed," Maggie said. Her sea-green eyes met mine and held the gaze until I looked away. Come on, Martha, I pleaded silently. Where are you when I need you?

Like an angel, Martha burst through the back door at that very moment. It took her less than a second to size up the situation, and her eyes went from wry amusement to compassion when she saw the agony on my face. She swept forward and blessedly took control.

"Well, if it isn't the elusive Ms. Trinidad," she said, pulling Erica into an easy embrace. "I thought Southern California had swallowed you up."

Erica had the good grace to look chagrined. "I, uh, got pretty busy out there," she stammered. It did my heart good to see her cringe under Martha's scrutiny.

"I guess you must have," Martha went on, her eyes smiling, giving no outward sign that she was ticked off. "What's it been, nine, ten months?"

"Nine months, three weeks and four days," Erica said, looking directly at me. My insides did another flipflop, and I felt the blush creep back over my face.

"Erica's a famous author," Martha went on, smiling at Maggie. "She's been making a movie with that other famous woman, the movie director. What's her name?"

Erica's face turned crimson beneath her deep tan, but she smiled at Martha, acknowledging the fairness of the jab. "Her name is Marie Jacobson," she said. "It was an interesting experience, working with her. But I'm glad it's finally over. Movie-making is stressful. Besides, I missed my life." She said this last part looking pointedly at me.

"Hmmm," Martha intoned.

I had been struck completely dumb since Erica's arrival, and Maggie was looking at me with something between amusement and concern. Everyone seemed to be handling this a lot better than I was.

"So, Erica, why don't you come on out back,"

Martha said, taking Erica by the elbow. "I'll introduce you around." To me it looked like Martha was applying a tad more pressure to the elbow than was absolutely necessary.

"Well, I didn't mean to crash a party," Erica said, sounding uncharacteristically unsure of herself. "I guess I should have called."

"Yes, you probably should have," I barely heard Martha say into Erica's ear, "About nine months ago."

Maggie and I were left alone, the entryway suddenly seeming quite close. She handed me the wine glass she'd brought me and I nodded my thanks. I held it to my face, feeling the cool glass against my hot skin. Maggie's eyes were burning into me.

"How long were you lovers?" she asked, sipping her own wine. She leaned against the wall and I studied her face. I could drown in those eyes, I thought, if I let myself.

"Not very long," I said. "She left for L.A. and I've been pretty much playing the fool ever since."

"You still love her," she said. It wasn't a question.

"I'm extremely mad at her," I said.

"And you love her," she repeated.

"She treated me like shit. I've never let anyone do that before." My voice sounded strangely far away.

"And you still love her."

I set my glass down and took two steps toward Maggie. I touched the velvety softness of her cheek, the satin of her soft curls. I leaned forward, touched her lips with mine, probed them gently until, with a small shudder, she opened her mouth to me and let

190

me kiss her deeply. My arms went around her waist and I let myself go, pulling her into me until our breathing became ragged and urgent.

"Cassidy," she said. It took me a while to catch my breath.

"What?" I asked, looking into her deep, lovely eyes.

"You don't have to prove yourself. I already know how you feel about me. The question I asked was, do you love Erica Trinidad?"

The tears had gathered in my eyes and began to slide down my cheeks, stinging the cuts on my face. I welcomed the pain, deserving it, wishing it were worse. It was the most miserable syllable I'd ever muttered, the lousiest sound I'd ever made. But Maggie's eyes held mine, forcing me to tell her the truth.

"Yes," I said, hating myself for it. "Yes," I repeated, letting the tears fall freely. "Yes, God help me, I think I do." I rarely cried and Maggie held me, letting me get it out, not uncomfortable with my wretched display of emotion. When at last I was able to pull myself away, there were tears in her eyes too.

"It's okay," she said, wiping her eyes. "One way or another, we'll get through this. Just keep being honest with me, okay?" She kissed my cheek and wiped away some of the wetness from my face. "Keep in touch," she said, turning for the door.

"Please Maggie," I said miserably. "Don't walk out now."

"Hey, babe." There was no unkindness in her voice. "I'm a lot of things, including wonderfully understanding and mature." An ironic smile played at the corners of her mouth. "But I've never been big on playing second fiddle."

Her reference to Herman Hugh made me grimace, but before I could say a word, she went on.

"Besides," she smiled, "you know where I'll be."

I watched her leave, a lump the size of a grapefruit lodged in my throat. She shouldn't *have* to play second fiddle, I thought, my tears turning to anger as I watched her boat disappear around the tip of the island. And then another thought entered my head, and I started to smile. I shouldn't have to play second fiddle either. And right then and there I knew that neither of us was going to.

I grabbed my boat keys and ran as fast as I could down the ramp to the dock. My Sea Swirl was faster than her rental boat, and if I gunned it, I'd be able to catch her before she made it back to the marina.

A few of the publications of
THE NAIAD PRESS, INC.
P.O. Box 10543 • Tallahassee, Florida 32302
Phone (904) 539-5965
Toll-Free Order Number: 1-800-533-1973
Mail orders welcome. Please include 15% postage.
Write or call for our free catalog which also features an
incredible selection of lesbian videos.

COSTA BRAVA by Marta Balletbo Coll. 144 pp. Read the book,
see the movie! ISBN 1-56280-153-8 $11.95

MEETING MAGDALENE & OTHER STORIES by
Marilyn Freeman. 144 pp. Read the book, see the movie!
ISBN 1-56280-170-8 11.95

SECOND FIDDLE by Kate Calloway. 208 pp. P.I. Cassidy James'
second case. ISBN 1-56280-169-6 11.95

LAUREL by Isabel Miller. 128 pp. By the author of the beloved
Patience and Sarah. ISBN 1-56280-146-5 10.95

LOVE OR MONEY by Jackie Calhoun. 240 pp. The romance of
real life. ISBN 1-56280-147-3 10.95

SMOKE AND MIRRORS by Pat Welch. 224 pp. 5th Helen Black
Mystery. ISBN 1-56280-143-0 10.95

DANCING IN THE DARK edited by Barbara Grier & Christine
Cassidy. 272 pp. Erotic love stories by Naiad Press authors.
ISBN 1-56280-144-9 14.95

TIME AND TIME AGAIN by Catherine Ennis. 176 pp. Passionate
love affair. ISBN 1-56280-145-7 10.95

PAXTON COURT by Diane Salvatore. 256 pp. Erotic and wickedly
funny contemporary tale about the business of learning to live
together. ISBN 1-56280-114-7 10.95

INNER CIRCLE by Claire McNab. 208 pp. 8th Carol Ashton
Mystery. ISBN 1-56280-135-X 10.95

LESBIAN SEX: AN ORAL HISTORY by Susan Johnson.
240 pp. Need we say more? ISBN 1-56280-142-2 14.95

BABY, IT'S COLD by Jaye Maiman. 256 pp. 5th Robin Miller
Mystery. ISBN 1-56280-141-4 19.95

WILD THINGS by Karin Kallmaker. 240 pp. By the undisputed
mistress of lesbian romance. ISBN 1-56280-139-2 10.95

THE GIRL NEXT DOOR by Mindy Kaplan. 208 pp. Just what
you'd expect. ISBN 1-56280-140-6 10.95

NOW AND THEN by Penny Hayes. 240 pp. Romance on the
westward journey. ISBN 1-56280-121-X 10.95

HEART ON FIRE by Diana Simmonds. 176 pp. The romantic and
erotic rival of *Curious Wine*. ISBN 1-56280-152-X 10.95

DEATH AT LAVENDER BAY by Lauren Wright Douglas. 208 pp.
1st Allison O'Neil Mystery. ISBN 1-56280-085-X 10.95

YES I SAID YES I WILL by Judith McDaniel. 272 pp. Hot
romance by famous author. ISBN 1-56280-138-4 10.95

FORBIDDEN FIRES by Margaret C. Anderson. Edited by Mathilda
Hills. 176 pp. Famous author's "unpublished" Lesbian romance.
ISBN 1-56280-123-6 21.95

SIDE TRACKS by Teresa Stores. 160 pp. Gender-bending
Lesbians on the road. ISBN 1-56280-122-8 10.95

HOODED MURDER by Annette Van Dyke. 176 pp. 1st Jessie
Batelle Mystery. ISBN 1-56280-134-1 10.95

WILDWOOD FLOWERS by Julia Watts. 208 pp. Hilarious and
heart-warming tale of true love. ISBN 1-56280-127-9 10.95

NEVER SAY NEVER by Linda Hill. 224 pp. Rule #1: Never get involved
with . . . ISBN 1-56280-126-0 10.95

THE SEARCH by Melanie McAllester. 240 pp. Exciting top cop
Tenny Mendoza case. ISBN 1-56280-150-3 10.95

THE WISH LIST by Saxon Bennett. 192 pp. Romance through
the years. ISBN 1-56280-125-2 10.95

FIRST IMPRESSIONS by Kate Calloway. 208 pp. P.I. Cassidy
James' first case. ISBN 1-56280-133-3 10.95

OUT OF THE NIGHT by Kris Bruyer. 192 pp. Spine-tingling
thriller. ISBN 1-56280-120-1 10.95

NORTHERN BLUE by Tracey Richardson. 224 pp. Police recruits
Miki & Miranda — passion in the line of fire. ISBN 1-56280-118-X 10.95

LOVE'S HARVEST by Peggy J. Herring. 176 pp. by the author of
Once More With Feeling. ISBN 1-56280-117-1 10.95

THE COLOR OF WINTER by Lisa Shapiro. 208 pp. Romantic
love beyond your wildest dreams. ISBN 1-56280-116-3 10.95

FAMILY SECRETS by Laura DeHart Young. 208 pp. Enthralling
romance and suspense. ISBN 1-56280-119-8 10.95

INLAND PASSAGE by Jane Rule. 288 pp. Tales exploring conven-
tional & unconventional relationships. ISBN 0-930044-56-8 10.95

DOUBLE BLUFF by Claire McNab. 208 pp. 7th Carol Ashton
Mystery. ISBN 1-56280-096-5 10.95

BAR GIRLS by Lauran Hoffman. 176 pp. See the movie, read
the book!   ISBN 1-56280-115-5   10.95

THE FIRST TIME EVER edited by Barbara Grier & Christine
Cassidy. 272 pp. Love stories by Naiad Press authors.
                                        ISBN 1-56280-086-8   14.95

MISS PETTIBONE AND MISS McGRAW by Brenda Weathers.
208 pp. A charming ghostly love story. ISBN 1-56280-151-1   10.95

CHANGES by Jackie Calhoun. 208 pp. Involved romance and
relationships.   ISBN 1-56280-083-3   10.95

FAIR PLAY by Rose Beecham. 256 pp. 3rd Amanda Valentine
Mystery.   ISBN 1-56280-081-7   10.95

PAYBACK by Celia Cohen. 176 pp. A gripping thriller of romance,
revenge and betrayal.   ISBN 1-56280-084-1   10.95

THE BEACH AFFAIR by Barbara Johnson. 224 pp. Sizzling
summer romance/mystery/intrigue.   ISBN 1-56280-090-6   10.95

GETTING THERE by Robbi Sommers. 192 pp. Nobody does it
like Robbi!   ISBN 1-56280-099-X   10.95

FINAL CUT by Lisa Haddock. 208 pp. 2nd Carmen Ramirez
Mystery.   ISBN 1-56280-088-4   10.95

FLASHPOINT by Katherine V. Forrest. 256 pp. A Lesbian
blockbuster!   ISBN 1-56280-079-5   10.95

CLAIRE OF THE MOON by Nicole Conn. Audio Book —Read
by Marianne Hyatt.   ISBN 1-56280-113-9   16.95

FOR LOVE AND FOR LIFE: INTIMATE PORTRAITS OF
LESBIAN COUPLES by Susan Johnson. 224 pp.
                                        ISBN 1-56280-091-4   14.95

DEVOTION by Mindy Kaplan. 192 pp. See the movie — read
the book!   ISBN 1-56280-093-0   10.95

SOMEONE TO WATCH by Jaye Maiman. 272 pp. 4th Robin
Miller Mystery.   ISBN 1-56280-095-7   10.95

GREENER THAN GRASS by Jennifer Fulton. 208 pp. A young
woman — a stranger in her bed.   ISBN 1-56280-092-2   10.95

TRAVELS WITH DIANA HUNTER by Regine Sands. Erotic
lesbian romp. Audio Book (2 cassettes) ISBN 1-56280-107-4   16.95

CABIN FEVER by Carol Schmidt. 256 pp. Sizzling suspense
and passion.   ISBN 1-56280-089-1   10.95

THERE WILL BE NO GOODBYES by Laura DeHart Young. 192
pp. Romantic love, strength, and friendship.   ISBN 1-56280-103-1   10.95

FAULTLINE by Sheila Ortiz Taylor. 144 pp. Joyous comic
lesbian novel.   ISBN 1-56280-108-2   9.95

OPEN HOUSE by Pat Welch. 176 pp. 4th Helen Black Mystery.
                                        ISBN 1-56280-102-3   10.95

ONCE MORE WITH FEELING by Peggy J. Herring. 240 pp. Lighthearted, loving romantic adventure. ISBN 1-56280-089-2 10.95

FOREVER by Evelyn Kennedy. 224 pp. Passionate romance — love overcoming all obstacles. ISBN 1-56280-094-9 10.95

WHISPERS by Kris Bruyer. 176 pp. Romantic ghost story
ISBN 1-56280-082-5 10.95

NIGHT SONGS by Penny Mickelbury. 224 pp. 2nd Gianna Maglione Mystery. ISBN 1-56280-097-3 10.95

GETTING TO THE POINT by Teresa Stores. 256 pp. Classic southern Lesbian novel. ISBN 1-56280-100-7 10.95

PAINTED MOON by Karin Kallmaker. 224 pp. Delicious Kallmaker romance. ISBN 1-56280-075-2 10.95

THE MYSTERIOUS NAIAD edited by Katherine V. Forrest & Barbara Grier. 320 pp. Love stories by Naiad Press authors.
ISBN 1-56280-074-4 14.95

DAUGHTERS OF A CORAL DAWN by Katherine V. Forrest. 240 pp. Tenth Anniversay Edition. ISBN 1-56280-104-X 10.95

BODY GUARD by Claire McNab. 208 pp. 6th Carol Ashton Mystery. ISBN 1-56280-073-6 10.95

CACTUS LOVE by Lee Lynch. 192 pp. Stories by the beloved storyteller. ISBN 1-56280-071-X 9.95

SECOND GUESS by Rose Beecham. 216 pp. 2nd Amanda Valentine Mystery. ISBN 1-56280-069-8 9.95

A RAGE OF MAIDENS by Lauren Wright Douglas. 240 pp. 6th Caitlin Reece Mystery. ISBN 1-56280-068-X 10.95

TRIPLE EXPOSURE by Jackie Calhoun. 224 pp. Romantic drama involving many characters. ISBN 1-56280-067-1 10.95

UP, UP AND AWAY by Catherine Ennis. 192 pp. Delightful romance. ISBN 1-56280-065-5 9.95

PERSONAL ADS by Robbi Sommers. 176 pp. Sizzling short stories. ISBN 1-56280-059-0 10.95

CROSSWORDS by Penny Sumner. 256 pp. 2nd Victoria Cross Mystery. ISBN 1-56280-064-7 9.95

SWEET CHERRY WINE by Carol Schmidt. 224 pp. A novel of suspense. ISBN 1-56280-063-9 9.95

CERTAIN SMILES by Dorothy Tell. 160 pp. Erotic short stories.
ISBN 1-56280-066-3 9.95

EDITED OUT by Lisa Haddock. 224 pp. 1st Carmen Ramirez Mystery. ISBN 1-56280-077-9 9.95

WEDNESDAY NIGHTS by Camarin Grae. 288 pp. Sexy adventure. ISBN 1-56280-060-4 10.95

SMOKEY O by Celia Cohen. 176 pp. Relationships on the
playing field.   ISBN 1-56280-057-4   9.95

KATHLEEN O'DONALD by Penny Hayes. 256 pp. Rose and
Kathleen find each other and employment in 1909 NYC.
                                            ISBN 1-56280-070-1   9.95

STAYING HOME by Elisabeth Nonas. 256 pp. Molly and Alix
want a baby . . . or do they?   ISBN 1-56280-076-0   10.95

TRUE LOVE by Jennifer Fulton. 240 pp. Six lesbians searching
for love in all the "right" places.   ISBN 1-56280-035-3   10.95

KEEPING SECRETS by Penny Mickelbury. 208 pp. 1st Gianna
Maglione Mystery.   ISBN 1-56280-052-3   9.95

THE ROMANTIC NAIAD edited by Katherine V. Forrest &
Barbara Grier. 336 pp. Love stories by Naiad Press authors.
                                            ISBN 1-56280-054-X   14.95

UNDER MY SKIN by Jaye Maiman. 336 pp. 3rd Robin Miller
Mystery.   ISBN 1-56280-049-3.   10.95

CAR POOL by Karin Kallmaker. 272pp. Lesbians on wheels
and then some!   ISBN 1-56280-048-5   10.95

NOT TELLING MOTHER: STORIES FROM A LIFE by Diane
Salvatore. 176 pp. Her 3rd novel.   ISBN 1-56280-044-2   9.95

GOBLIN MARKET by Lauren Wright Douglas. 240pp. 5th Caitlin
Reece Mystery.   ISBN 1-56280-047-7   10.95

LONG GOODBYES by Nikki Baker. 256 pp. 3rd Virginia Kelly
Mystery.   ISBN 1-56280-042-6   9.95

FRIENDS AND LOVERS by Jackie Calhoun. 224 pp. Mid-
western Lesbian lives and loves.   ISBN 1-56280-041-8   10.95

THE CAT CAME BACK by Hilary Mullins. 208 pp. Highly
praised Lesbian novel.   ISBN 1-56280-040-X   9.95

BEHIND CLOSED DOORS by Robbi Sommers. 192 pp. Hot,
erotic short stories.   ISBN 1-56280-039-6   9.95

CLAIRE OF THE MOON by Nicole Conn. 192 pp. See the
movie — read the book!   ISBN 1-56280-038-8   10.95

SILENT HEART by Claire McNab. 192 pp. Exotic Lesbian
romance.   ISBN 1-56280-036-1   10.95

THE SPY IN QUESTION by Amanda Kyle Williams. 256 pp.
4th Madison McGuire Mystery.   ISBN 1-56280-037-X   9.95

SAVING GRACE by Jennifer Fulton. 240 pp. Adventure and
romantic entanglement.   ISBN 1-56280-051-5   10.95

CURIOUS WINE by Katherine V. Forrest. 176 pp. Tenth Anniver-
sary Edition. The most popular contemporary Lesbian love story.
                                            ISBN 1-56280-053-1   10.95
        Audio Book (2 cassettes)   ISBN 1-56280-105-8   16.95

CHAUTAUQUA by Catherine Ennis. 192 pp. Exciting, romantic
adventure.   ISBN 1-56280-032-9   9.95

A PROPER BURIAL by Pat Welch. 192 pp. 3rd Helen Black
Mystery.   ISBN 1-56280-033-7   9.95

SILVERLAKE HEAT: A Novel of Suspense by Carol Schmidt.
240 pp. Rhonda is as hot as Laney's dreams.   ISBN 1-56280-031-0   9.95

LOVE, ZENA BETH by Diane Salvatore. 224 pp. The most talked
about lesbian novel of the nineties!   ISBN 1-56280-030-2   10.95

A DOORYARD FULL OF FLOWERS by Isabel Miller. 160 pp.
Stories incl. 2 sequels to *Patience and Sarah*.   ISBN 1-56280-029-9   9.95

MURDER BY TRADITION by Katherine V. Forrest. 288 pp. 4th
Kate Delafield Mystery.   ISBN 1-56280-002-7   11.95

THE EROTIC NAIAD edited by Katherine V. Forrest & Barbara
Grier. 224 pp. Love stories by Naiad Press authors.
                                                   ISBN 1-56280-026-4   14.95

DEAD CERTAIN by Claire McNab. 224 pp. 5th Carol Ashton
Mystery.   ISBN 1-56280-027-2   10.95

CRAZY FOR LOVING by Jaye Maiman. 320 pp. 2nd Robin Miller
Mystery.   ISBN 1-56280-025-6   10.95

STONEHURST by Barbara Johnson. 176 pp. Passionate regency
romance.   ISBN 1-56280-024-8   9.95

INTRODUCING AMANDA VALENTINE by Rose Beecham.
256 pp. 1st Amanda Valentine Mystery.   ISBN 1-56280-021-3   10.95

UNCERTAIN COMPANIONS by Robbi Sommers. 204 pp.
Steamy, erotic novel.   ISBN 1-56280-017-5   9.95

A TIGER'S HEART by Lauren W. Douglas. 240 pp. 4th Caitlin
Reece Mystery.   ISBN 1-56280-018-3   9.95

PAPERBACK ROMANCE by Karin Kallmaker. 256 pp. A
delicious romance.   ISBN 1-56280-019-1   10.95

THE LAVENDER HOUSE MURDER by Nikki Baker. 224 pp.
2nd Virginia Kelly Mystery.   ISBN 1-56280-012-4   9.95

PASSION BAY by Jennifer Fulton. 224 pp. Passionate romance,
virgin beaches, tropical skies.   ISBN 1-56280-028-0   10.95

STICKS AND STONES by Jackie Calhoun. 208 pp. Contemporary
lesbian lives and loves.   ISBN 1-56280-020-5   9.95
Audio Book (2 cassettes)   ISBN 1-56280-106-6   16.95

UNDER THE SOUTHERN CROSS by Claire McNab. 192 pp.
Romantic nights Down Under.   ISBN 1-56280-011-6   9.95

GRASSY FLATS by Penny Hayes. 256 pp. Lesbian romance in
the '30s.   ISBN 1-56280-010-8   9.95

A SINGULAR SPY by Amanda K. Williams. 192 pp. 3rd
Madison McGuire Mystery.   ISBN 1-56280-008-6   8.95

THE END OF APRIL by Penny Sumner. 240 pp. 1st Victoria
Cross Mystery.   ISBN 1-56280-007-8   8.95

KISS AND TELL by Robbi Sommers. 192 pp. Scorching stories
by the author of *Pleasures.*   ISBN 1-56280-005-1   10.95

STILL WATERS by Pat Welch. 208 pp. 2nd Helen Black Mystery.
                                        ISBN 0-941483-97-5   9.95

TO LOVE AGAIN by Evelyn Kennedy. 208 pp. Wildly romantic
love story.   ISBN 0-941483-85-1   9.95

IN THE GAME by Nikki Baker. 192 pp. 1st Virginia Kelly
Mystery.   ISBN 1-56280-004-3   9.95

STRANDED by Camarin Grae. 320 pp. Entertaining, riveting
adventure.   ISBN 0-941483-99-1   9.95

THE DAUGHTERS OF ARTEMIS by Lauren Wright Douglas.
240 pp. 3rd Caitlin Reece Mystery.   ISBN 0-941483-95-9   9.95

CLEARWATER by Catherine Ennis. 176 pp. Romantic secrets
of a small Louisiana town.   ISBN 0-941483-65-7   8.95

THE HALLELUJAH MURDERS by Dorothy Tell. 176 pp. 2nd
Poppy Dillworth Mystery.   ISBN 0-941483-88-6   8.95

SECOND CHANCE by Jackie Calhoun. 256 pp. Contemporary
Lesbian lives and loves.   ISBN 0-941483-93-2   9.95

BENEDICTION by Diane Salvatore. 272 pp. Striking, contemporary romantic novel.   ISBN 0-941483-90-8   10.95

TOUCHWOOD by Karin Kallmaker. 240 pp. Loving, May/
December romance.   ISBN 0-941483-76-2   9.95

COP OUT by Claire McNab. 208 pp. 4th Carol Ashton Mystery.
                                        ISBN 0-941483-84-3   10.95

THE BEVERLY MALIBU by Katherine V. Forrest. 288 pp. 3rd
Kate Delafield Mystery.   ISBN 0-941483-48-7   11.95

THE PROVIDENCE FILE by Amanda Kyle Williams. 256 pp.
2nd Madison McGuire Mystery.   ISBN 0-941483-92-4   8.95

I LEFT MY HEART by Jaye Maiman. 320 pp. 1st Robin Miller
Mystery.   ISBN 0-941483-72-X   10.95

THE PRICE OF SALT by Patricia Highsmith (writing as Claire
Morgan). 288 pp. Classic lesbian novel, first issued in 1952 . . .
acknowledged by its author under her own, very famous, name.
                                        ISBN 1-56280-003-5   10.95

SIDE BY SIDE by Isabel Miller. 256 pp. From beloved author of
Patience and Sarah.   ISBN 0-941483-77-0   10.95

STAYING POWER: LONG TERM LESBIAN COUPLES by
Susan E. Johnson. 352 pp. Joys of coupledom. ISBN 0-941-483-75-4 14.95

SLICK by Camarin Grae. 304 pp. Exotic, erotic adventure.
                                        ISBN 0-941483-74-6   9.95

NINTH LIFE by Lauren Wright Douglas. 256 pp. 2nd Caitlin
Reece Mystery. ISBN 0-941483-50-9   9.95

PLAYERS by Robbi Sommers. 192 pp. Sizzling, erotic novel.
ISBN 0-941483-73-8   9.95

MURDER AT RED ROOK RANCH by Dorothy Tell. 224 pp.
1st Poppy Dillworth Mystery. ISBN 0-941483-80-0   8.95

A ROOM FULL OF WOMEN by Elisabeth Nonas. 256 pp.
Contemporary Lesbian lives. ISBN 0-941483-69-X   9.95

THEME FOR DIVERSE INSTRUMENTS by Jane Rule. 208 pp.
Powerful romantic lesbian stories. ISBN 0-941483-63-0   8.95

CLUB 12 by Amanda Kyle Williams. 288 pp. Espionage thriller
featuring a lesbian agent! ISBN 0-941483-64-9   9.95

DEATH DOWN UNDER by Claire McNab. 240 pp. 3rd Carol
Ashton Mystery. ISBN 0-941483-39-8   10.95

MONTANA FEATHERS by Penny Hayes. 256 pp. Vivian and
Elizabeth find love in frontier Montana. ISBN 0-941483-61-4   9.95

LIFESTYLES by Jackie Calhoun. 224 pp. Contemporary Lesbian
lives and loves. ISBN 0-941483-57-6   10.95

WILDERNESS TREK by Dorothy Tell. 192 pp. Six women on
vacation learning "new" skills. ISBN 0-941483-60-6   8.95

MURDER BY THE BOOK by Pat Welch. 256 pp. 1st Helen
Black Mystery. ISBN 0-941483-59-2   9.95

THERE'S SOMETHING I'VE BEEN MEANING TO TELL YOU
Ed. by Loralee MacPike. 288 pp. Gay men and lesbians coming out
to their children. ISBN 0-941483-44-4   9.95

LIFTING BELLY by Gertrude Stein. Ed. by Rebecca Mark. 104 pp.
Erotic poetry. ISBN 0-941483-51-7   10.95

AFTER THE FIRE by Jane Rule. 256 pp. Warm, human novel by
this incomparable author. ISBN 0-941483-45-2   8.95

PLEASURES by Robbi Sommers. 204 pp. Unprecedented
eroticism. ISBN 0-941483-49-5   9.95

EDGEWISE by Camarin Grae. 372 pp. Spellbinding
adventure. ISBN 0-941483-19-3   9.95

FATAL REUNION by Claire McNab. 224 pp. 2nd Carol Ashton
Mystery. ISBN 0-941483-40-1   10.95

These are just a few of the many Naiad Press titles — we are the oldest and
largest lesbian/feminist publishing company in the world. We also offer an
enormous selection of lesbian video products. Please request a complete
catalog. We offer personal service; we encourage and welcome direct mail
orders from individuals who have limited access to bookstores carrying our
publications.